The Beginning Place

Books by Ursula K. Le Guin

Novels

THE BEGINNING PLACE
MALAFRENA
VERY FAR AWAY FROM ANYWHERE ELSE
THE WORD FOR WORLD IS FOREST
THE DISPOSSESSED
THE LATHE OF HEAVEN
THE FARTHEST SHORE
THE TOMBS OF ATUAN
A WIZARD OF EARTHSEA
THE LEFT HAND OF DARKNESS
CITY OF ILLUSIONS
PLANET OF EXILE
ROCANNON'S WORLD

Short Stories

ORSINIAN TALES
THE WIND'S TWELVE QUARTERS

For Children

LEESE WEBSTER

Poetry and Criticism

THE LANGUAGE OF THE NIGHT
FROM ELFLAND TO POUGHKEEPSIE
WILD ANGELS

The Beginning Place

Ursula K. Le Guin

HARPER & ROW, PUBLISHERS
NEW YORK

Cambridge		London
Hagerstown		Mexico City
Philadelphia		São Paulo
San Francisco		Sydney

1817

Designer: Stephanie Winkler

Library of Congress Cataloging in Publication Data

Le Guin, Ursula K   DATE
    The beginning place.
    I. Title.
PZ4.L518Be   1980   [PB3562.B42]   813'.5'4   79–2653
ISBN 0–06–012573–X

Qué río es ésta
por el cual corre el Ganges?

—J. L. Borges: *Heráclito*

1

"Checker on Seven!" and back between the checkstands unloading the wire carts, apples three for eighty-nine, pineapple chunks on special, half gallon of two percent, seventy-five, four, and one is five, thank you, from ten to six six days a week; and he was good at it. The manager, a man made of iron filings and bile, complimented him on his efficiency. The other checkers, older, married, talked baseball, football, mortgages, orthodontists. They called him Rodge, except Donna, who called him Buck. Customers at rush times were hands giving money, taking money. At slow times old men and women liked to talk, it didn't matter much what you answered, they didn't listen. Efficiency got him through the job daily but not beyond it. Eight hours a day of chicken noodle two for sixty-nine, dog chow on special, half pint of Derry Wip, ninety-five, one, and five is forty. He walked back to Oak Valley Road and had dinner with his mother and watched some television and went to bed. Sometimes he wondered what he would be doing if Sam's Thrift-E-Mart had been on the other side of the freeway, for there was no pedestrian crossing for four blocks on one side and six on the other, and he never would have got to the place. But he had driven there to stock up the refrigerator the day after they moved in, and saw the sign CHECKER WANTED, which had been up for one half hour. If he hadn't fallen into the job he might have gone ahead and bought a car so that he could work downtown, as he had planned. But it wouldn't have been much of a car, whereas now he was saving enough to amount to something when the time came. He would rather live in town and get along without a car of his own but his mother was afraid of inner cities. He looked at cars as he walked home and considered what kind he might get when the time came. He was not very interested in cars, but since he had given up the idea of school he would have to spend the money on something, finally, and his mind always fell into the same habit, as he walked home; he was tired, and all day he had handled things for sale and the money that bought them, until his mind held nothing else because his hands never held anything else, and yet kept none of it.

In early spring when they first moved here the sky above the roofs had flared cold green and gold as he walked home. Now in summer the treeless streets were still bright and hot at seven. Planes gaining altitude from the airport ten miles south cut the thick, glaring sky, dragging their sound and shadow; broken swings of painted steel play-gyms screeched beside the driveways. The development was named Kensington Heights. To get to Oak Valley Road he crossed Loma Linda Drive, Raleigh Drive, Pine View Place, turned onto Kensington Avenue, crossed Chelsea Oaks Road. There were no heights, no valleys, no Raleighs, no oaks. On Oak Valley Road the houses were two-story six-unit apartment houses painted brown and white. Between the carports were patches of lawn with edgings of crushed white rock planted with juniper. Gum wrappers, soft-drink cans, plastic lids, the indestructible shells and skeletons of the perishables he handled at the counters of the grocery, lay among the white rocks and the dark plants. On Raleigh Drive and Pine View Place the houses were duplexes and on Loma Linda Drive they were separate dwellings, each with its own driveway, carport, lawn, white rocks, juniper. The sidewalks were even, the streets level, the land flat. The old city, downtown, was built on hills above a river, but all its eastern and northern suburbs were flat. The only view he had seen out here had been on the day they drove in from the east with the U-Haul. Just before the city limits sign there was some kind of viaduct the freeway went over, and you looked down over fields. Beyond them the city in a golden haze. Fields, meadows in that soft evening light, and the shadows of trees. Then a paint factory with its many-colored sign facing the freeway, and the housing developments began.

One evening after work, a hot evening, he crossed the wide parking lot of Sam's Thrift-E-Mart and went up the exit ramp onto the narrow sidewalk rim of the freeway to see if he could walk back, walk out into the country, the fields he had seen, but there was no way. Rubbish of paper and metal and plastic underfoot, the air lashed and staggering with suction winds and the ground shuddering as each truck approached and passed, eardrums battered by noise and nothing to breathe but burnt rubber and diesel fumes. He gave it up after half an hour and tried to get off the freeway, but the suburban streets were divided from the freeway embankment by chainlink fence. He had to go clear back and across the Thrift-E-Mart parking lot to get to Kensington Avenue. The defeat left him shaky and angry, as if he had been assaulted. He walked home squinting in the hot level sunlight. His mother's car wasn't in the carport. The telephone was ringing as he let himself in.

"There you are! I've been calling and calling. Where were you? I called twice already before this call. I'll be here until about ten. At Durbina's. There's a turkey dinner in the freezer. Don't use the Oriental Menu dinners, they're for Wednesday. There's a Mixon's Turkey Dinner." $1.29, his head rang it up, thank you. "I'm going to miss the beginning

3

of that movie on Channel Six, you watch it for me till I get home."

"O.K."

"Byebye then."

"Bye."

"Hugh?"

"Yes."

"What kept you so late?"

"Walked home a different way."

"You sound so cross."

"I don't know."

"Take some aspirin. And a cold shower. It's so hot. That's what I'd like. But I won't be late. Take care now. You're not going out, are you?"

"No."

She hesitated, said nothing, but did not hang up the phone. He said, "Bye," and hung up, and stood beside the telephone stand. He felt heavy, a heavy animal, a thick, wrinkled creature with its lower lip hanging open and feet like truck tires. Why are you fifteen minutes late why are you cross take care don't eat the frozen Oriental Menu don't go out. All right. Take care take care. He went and put the Mixon's Turkey Dinner into the oven although he had not preheated the oven as the directions said to do, and set the timer. He was hungry. He was always hungry. He was never exactly hungry, but always wanting to eat. There was a bag of peanuts in the pantry cupboard; he took the bag into the living room and turned on the television set and sat down in the armchair. The chair shook and creaked under his weight. He got up again suddenly, dropping the bag of peanuts he had just opened. It was too much, the elephant feeding itself peanuts. He could feel his mouth hanging open, because he could not seem to get air into his lungs. His throat was closed off by something in it trying to get out. He stood there beside the armchair, his body trembling in a jerky way, and the thing in his throat came out in words. "I can't, I can't," it said loudly.

Very frightened, in panic, he made for the front door, wrenched it open, got out of the house before the thing could go on talking. The hot, late sunlight glared on white rocks, carports, cars, walls, swings, television aerials. He stood there trembling, his jaw working: the thing was trying to force his jaw open and speak again. He broke and ran.

Right down Oak Valley Road, left onto Pine View Place, right again, he did not know, he could not read the signs. He did not run often or easily. His feet hit the ground hard, in heavy shocks. Cars, carports, houses blurred to a bright pounding blindness which, as he ran on, reddened and darkened. Words behind his eyes said *You are running out of daylight.* Air came acid into his throat and lungs, burning, his breath made the noise of tearing paper. The darkness thickened like blood. The jolt of his gait grew harder yet, he was running down, downhill. He tried to hold back, to slow down, feeling the world slide and crumble under his feet, a multiple lithe touch brush across his face. He saw or smelled leaves, dark leaves, branches, dirt, earth, leafmold, and through the hammer of his heart and breath heard a loud continual music. He took a few shaky, shuffling steps, went forward onto hands and knees, and then down, belly down full length on earth and rock at the edge of running water.

When at last he sat up he did not feel that he had been asleep but still it was like waking, like waking from deep sleep in quietness, when the self belongs wholly to the self and nothing can move it, until one wakens further. At the root of the quietness was the music of the water. Under his hand sand slid over rock. As he sat up he felt the air come easily into his lungs, a cool air smelling of earth and rotten leaves and growing leaves, all the different kinds of weeds and grass and bushes and trees, the cold scent of water, the dark scent of dirt, a sweet tang that was familiar though he could not name it, all the odors mixed and yet distinct like the threads in a piece of cloth, proving the olfactory part of the brain to be alive and immense, with room though no name for every scent, aroma, perfume, and stink that made up this vast, dark, profoundly strange and familiar smell of a stream bank in late evening in summer in the country.

For he was in the country. He had no idea how far he had run, having no clear idea of how long a mile was, but he knew he had run clear out of streets, out of houses, off the edge of the paved world, onto dirt. Dark, slightly damp, uneven, complex again, complex beyond belief— moving one finger he touched grains of sand and soil, decayed leaves, pebbles, a larger rock half buried, roots. He had lain with his face against that dirt, on it, in it. His head swam a little. He drew a long breath, and pressed his open hands against the earth.

It was not dark yet. His eyes had grown accustomed, and he could see clearly, though the darker colors and all shadowed places were near the verge of night. The sky between the black, distinct branches overhead was colorless and without variation of brightness to show where the sun had set. There were no stars yet. The stream, twenty or thirty feet wide and full of boulders, was like a livelier piece of the sky, flashing and glimmering around its rocks. The open, sandy banks on both sides were light; only downstream where the trees grew thicker did the dusk gather heavy, blurring details.

He rubbed sand and dead leaf and spiderweb off his face and hair, feeling the light sting of a branch-cut under his eye. He leaned forward on his elbow, intent, and touched the water of the stream with the fingers of his left hand:

very lightly at first, his hand flat, as if touching the skin of an animal; then he put his hand into the water and felt the musculature of the currents press against his palm. Presently he leaned forward farther, bent his head down, and with both hands in the shallows at the sand's edge, drank.

The water was cold and tasted of the sky.

Hugh crouched there on the muddy sand, his head still bowed, with the taste that is no taste on his lips and in his mouth. He straightened his back slowly then until he was kneeling with head erect, his hands on his knees, motionless. What his mind had no words for his body understood entirely and with ease, and praised.

When that intensity which he understood as prayer lessened, ebbed, and resolved again into alert and manifold pleasure, he sat back on his heels, looking about him more keenly and methodically than at first.

Where north was, no telling, beneath the even, colorless sky; but he was certain that the suburbs, the freeway, the city all were directly behind him. The path he had been on came out there, between a big pine with reddish bark and a mass of high, large-leaved shrubs. Behind them the path went up steep and was lost to sight in the thick dusk under the trees.

The stream ran directly across the axis of that path, from right to left. He could see for a long way upstream along the farther bank as it wound among trees and boulders and finally began to shelve higher above the water. Downstream the woods dropped away in increasing darkness broken by the slipping glimmer of the stream. Above the shore on both sides of the water, close by, the banks rose and then leveled into a clearing free of trees, a glade, almost a little meadow, grassy and much interrupted by bushes and shrubs.

The familiar smell he could not put a name to had grown stronger, his hand smelled of it—mint, that was it. The patch of weeds at the water's edge where he had put his hands down must be wild mint. He picked off a leaf and smelled it, then bit it, expecting it to be sweet like mint candy. It was pungent, slightly hairy, earthy, cold.

This is a good place, Hugh thought. And I got here. I finally got somewhere. I made it.

Behind his back the dinner in the oven, timer set, television gabbling to an empty room. The front door unlocked. Maybe not even shut. How long?

Mother coming home at ten.

Where were you, Hugh? Out for a walk But you weren't *home* when I got *home* you know how I Yes it got later than I thought I'm sorry But you weren't *home*—

He was on his feet already. But the mint leaf was in his mouth, his hands were wet, his shirt and jeans were a mess of leaves and muddy sand, and his heart was not troubled. I found the place, so I can come back to it, he said to himself.

He stood a minute longer listening to the water on the stones and watching the stillness of the branches against the evening sky; then set off back the way he had come, up the path between the high bushes and the pine. The way was steep and dark at first, then leveled out among sparse woods. It was easy to follow, though the thorny arms of blackberry creepers tripped him up a couple of times in the fast-increasing dusk. An old ditch, grass-overgrown, not much more than a dip or wrinkle in the ground, was the boundary of the wood; across it he faced open fields. Clear across them in the distance was the queer shifting passing flicker of carlights on the freeway. There were stationary lights to the right. He headed towards them, across the fields of dry grass and hard ridged dirt, coming at last to a rise or bank at the top of which ran a gravel road. There was a big building, floodlit, off to the left near the freeway; down the road the other direction was what looked like a couple of farmhouses. One of them also had

8

a light rigged in the front yard, and he headed for that, feeling certain that was how he should go: down this road between the farmhouses. Past their auto graveyards and barking dogs there was a dark stretch of trees in rows, and then the first streetlight, the end of Chelsea Gardens Place, leading to Chelsea Gardens Avenue, and on into the heart of a housing development. He followed a memory unavailable to consciousness of how he had come when he was running, and street by street unerringly brought himself back to Kensington Heights, onto Pine View Place, onto Oak Valley Road, and to the front door of 14067½- C Oak Valley Road: which was shut.

The television set was vibrating with canned laughter. He turned it off, then heard the kitchen timer buzzing and hurried to turn it off. The kitchen clock said five to nine. The turkey dinner was withered in its little aluminum coffin. He tried to eat it but it was stone. He drank a quart of milk and ate four slices of bread and butter, a pint of blueberry yogurt, and two apples; he got the bag of peanuts from the living room floor and shelled and ate them, sitting at the dinette table in the kitchen, thinking. It had been a long walk home. He had not looked at his watch, but it must have taken pretty near an hour. And surely he had spent an hour or more by the stream; and it had taken him a while to get there, even if he had been running, he wasn't any four-minute miler. He would have sworn it was ten o'clock or even eleven, if the clock and his watch did not unanimously contradict him.

Never much of a one for argument, he gave it up. He finished the peanuts, moved into the living room, turned off the light, turned on the television, instantly turned it off again, and sat down in the armchair. The chair shook and creaked, but this time he was more aware of its inadequacy as an armchair than of his own clumsy weight. He felt good, after his run. He felt sorry for the poor sleazy, shoddy chair, instead of disgusted with himself. Why had

9

he run? Well, no need to go over that. He had never done anything else all his life. Run-and-hide Rogers. But to have run and got somewhere, that was new. He had never got anywhere before, no place to hide, no place to be. And then to fall over his own feet onto his face into a place like that, a wild, secret place. As if all the suburbs, the duplex development motorhome supermarket parking lot used cars carport swingset white rocks juniper imitation bacon bits special gum wrappers where in five different states he had lived the last seven years, as if all that was unimportant after all, not permanent, not the way life had to be, since just outside it, just past the edge of it, there was silence, loneliness, water running in twilight, the taste of mint.

You shouldn't have drunk the water. Sewage. Typhoid. Cholera . . . No! That was the first clean water I ever drank. I'll go back there and drink it any damned time I want.

The creek. Stream, they would call it in the states where he had been in high school, but the word "creek" came to him from farther back in the darkness of remembrance, a twilight word to suit the twilight water, the racing shift and glimmer that filled his mind. The walls of the room he sat in resonated faintly to the noises of a television program in the apartment overhead, and were streaked with light from the streetlamp through lace curtains and sometimes the dim wheeling of the headlights of a passing car. Within, beneath that restless, unsilent half-light was the quiet place, the creek. From thinking of it his mind drifted on to old currents of thought: If I went where I want to go, if I went out to the college here and talked to people, there might be student loans for library school, or if I save enough and got started maybe a scholarship—and from this further, like a boat drifting past the islands within sight of shore, moving into a remoter future dreamed of earlier, a building with wide and much-frequented steps, stairways within and grand rooms and high windows, people quiet, at work quietly, as much at home among the endless shelves of books as the thoughts in a mind are at home, the City Library on a fifth-grade school trip to celebrate National Book Week and the home and harbor of his longing.

"What are you doing sitting in the dark? Without the TV on? And the front door not locked! Why aren't the lights on? I thought nobody was here." And when that had been talked about she found the turkey dinner, which he had not jammed far enough down into the garbage pail under the sink. "What did you eat? What on earth was wrong with it? Can't you read the directions? You must be taking the flu, you'd better take some aspirin. Really, Hugh, you just can't seem to look after yourself at all, you cannot manage the simplest thing. How can I be comfortable about going out after work to have a little time with my friends when you're so irresponsible? Where's the bag of peanuts I bought to take to Durbina's tomorrow?" And though at first he saw her, like the armchair, as simply inadequate, trying hard to do a job she wasn't up to, he could not keep seeing her from the quiet place but was drawn back, roped in, till all he could do was not listen, and say, "All right," and, after she had turned on the last commercial of the movie she had wanted to watch, "Good night, mother." And run and hide in bed.

At the small supermarket in the last city, where Hugh had first moved up from carrier to checker, things had been easygoing, with plenty of time for conversations or loafing around back in the stockrooms, but Sam's did heavy business, and each job was specialised and without relief. It might look like your line was going to finish with the next customer, but there was always another one coming. Hugh had learned how to think in bits and pieces, not a good method, but the only one available to him. During a working day he could get a certain amount of thinking done if he kept coming back to it; a thought would wait for him, like a patient dog, until he returned. His dog was waiting for him today when he woke up, and went to work with him, wagging its tail: He wanted to go back to the creek, to the place by the creek, and with time enough to stay a while. By ten-thirty, after checking through the old lady with an orthopedic shoe who always had to explain that canned salmon used to cost ten cents a can but now it was so outrageously overpriced because it was all being sent abroad on lend-lease to socialist countries, while she paid for her margarine and bread with food stamps, he had figured out that the best time to go to the creek place would be in the morning, not in the evening.

His mother and her new friend Durbina were studying some kind of occultism together, and lately she had been going to Durbina's at least once a week after work. That gave him a free evening; but only once a week, and he never knew which evening, and would have to worry about not getting home ahead of his mother.

She did not mind getting home before he did in daylight, but if she expected him to be there and he wasn't, or if she came home to an empty house in the dark, then it was no good. And lately it hadn't been good when she stayed alone in the house while it was getting dark. So there was no use trying to count on going out in the evening; it was like night school, no use thinking about it.

But in the morning, she left for work at eight. He could go to the creek place then. It was two hours, anyhow. In daylight there might be people around, he thought (in the afternoon, while Bill took over Seven to give him his break), there might be other people, or signs saying private property, no trespassing; but he would take the chance. It did not look like a place where many people came.

He was home at his usual time, quarter to seven, tonight,

but his mother did not come and there was no telephone call. He sat around reading the newspaper and wishing he had something to eat, like peanuts, the peanuts he had eaten last night that his mother had wanted to take to Durbina's tomorrow, that was tonight. Oh, hell, he thought, I could have gone to the creek place after all. He got up to go, but could not go now, not knowing when she would come back. He went to make himself dinner, but could find nothing he wanted; he ate bits and scraps, and made up and drank a can of frozen orange juice. He had a headache. He wanted a book to read, and thought, Why don't I get a car so I can drive downtown to the Library, why don't I go anywhere, why don't I have a car, but what was the use of a car if he worked from ten to six and had to stay home evenings? He watched a news-in-review show on television to shut out the dog of his mind that had turned on him and snarled, showing its teeth. The phone rang. His mother's voice was sharp. "I wanted to be sure before I started home this time," she said, and hung up.

In bed that night he tried to summon up images of solace, but they turned to torment; he fell back finally on a fantasy from years ago, a waitress he had used to see when he was fifteen. He imagined himself sucking her breasts, and so brought his masturbation to climax, and then lay desolate.

In the morning he got up at seven instead of eight. He had not told his mother that he was going to get up early. She did not like changes of routine. She sat with coffee cup and cigarette in the living room, the morning television news going, a frown between her penciled black eyebrows. She never had anything for breakfast but coffee. Hugh liked breakfast, he liked eggs, bacon, ham, toast, rolls, potatoes, sausage, grapefruit, orange juice, pancakes, yogurt, cereal, whatever; he put milk and sugar in his coffee. His mother found the sight, sounds, smells of his preparations sickening. There was no door between the kitchen area and the living-room area in this open-plan apartment. Hugh tried to move quietly, and did not fry anything, but it was no good. She came in past him where he sat at the dinette table trying to eat cornflakes noiselessly. She dropped her cup and saucer in the steel sink and said, "I'm going to work." He heard in her voice the terrible thin sound, a scraping sharpness, which he thought of (not in words) as the knife's edge. "All right," he said not turning, trying to make his voice soft, neutral, neuter; for he knew that it was his deep voice, his size, his big feet and thick fingers, his heavy, sexual body that she couldn't stand, that drove her to the edge.

She went straight out, though it was only twenty-five to eight. He heard the engine start, saw the blue Japanese car go past the picture window, going fast.

When he came to wash up at the sink he found her saucer chipped and the handle broken off the coffee cup. The small violence made his stomach turn over. He stood with his hands on the rim of the sink, his mouth open, swaying a little from foot to foot, a habit he had when distressed. He reached slowly forward, turned the cold water tap on, and let the water run. He watched it, the rush and stream and clarity of it, filling and overflowing the broken cup.

He washed the dishes, locked up, and set off. Right on Oak Valley, left on Pine View, and on. It was pleasant walking, the air sweet, the lid of the hot day not closed down yet. He got into a good swinging pace and after ten or twelve blocks had walked free of the grip of his mother's mood. But as he went on, checking his watch, he began to doubt that he could get to the creek place before he had to turn around and start back towards Sam's in order to get to work at ten. How had he got to the creek, stayed there, and come back, night before last, all in two hours? Maybe he was off course now, not going there by the short-

14

est way, or headed wrong altogether. The part of his mind that did not use words to think with ignored these doubts and worries, guiding him from street to street through about five miles of Kensington Heights and Sylvan Dell and Chelsea Gardens to the gravel road above the fields.

The big building near the freeway was the paint factory; from here you saw the back of its big many-colored sign. He went as far as the chainlink fence around its parking lot and looked down from the higher land there, trying to see the golden sunset fields he had seen from the car. In the morning light they had no glamour. Weedy, farmed once but no longer plowed or grazed, derelict. Waiting for the developers. A NO DUMPING sign stuck up out of a ditch full of thistles near the rusted chassis of a car. Far off across the fields clumps of trees cast their shadows westward; beyond them were the woods, rising blue in the smoggy, sunlit air. It was past eight-thirty, and getting hot.

Hugh took off his jeans jacket and wiped the sweat off his forehead and cheeks. He stood a minute looking towards the woodlands. If he went, even if he did no more than drink from the creek and leave at once, he would probably be late to work. He swore out loud, bitterly, and turned, and went back down the gravel road by the down-at-heel farmhouses and the tree nursery or Christmas tree lot or whatever it was, cut through to Chelsea Gardens Place, and walking steadily along the curved treeless streets between lawns, carports, houses, lawns, carports, houses, reached Sam's Thrift-E-Mart at ten minutes to ten. He was red-faced and sweaty, and Donna, in the stockroom, said, "You overslept, Buck."

Donna was about forty-five. She had a lot of dark red hair, which she had recently got made into a fashionable mane of curls and tendrils that made her look twenty from behind and sixty face on. She had a good figure, bad teeth, one bad son who drank, and one good son who drove in stock-car races. She liked Hugh and talked to him whenever

15

she got a chance, telling him—sometimes from checkstand to checkstand across the carts and customers—about the teeth, the sons, her husband's mother's cancer, her dog's pregnancy and its complications; she offered him puppies; they told each other the plots of movies and television shows. She had named him Buck his first day at work. "Buck Rogers in the twenty-first century, I bet you're too young to remember the real one," and she laughed at the paradox. This morning she said, "You overslept, Buck. Shame on you."

"I got up at seven," he countered.

"Then what you been running for? There's steam coming off you!"

He stood not knowing what to say, then gasped at the word. "Running," he said. "You know. Supposed to be good for you."

"Yeah, there was some besseller about that, wasn't there? Like jogging only a lot harder. What do you do, just run around the block ten times? or go to a gym or something?"

"I just sort of run," Hugh said, discomforted by meeting her sympathetic interest with a lie; yet it never entered his head to try to tell her about the place he had found by the creek. "I'm sort of overweight. I thought I'd try it."

"I guess you might be heavy for your age. You look fine to me," Donna said, looking him up and down. Hugh was profoundly pleased.

"I'm fat," he said, slapping his belly.

"A little podge, maybe. But look at all the bone you got to carry it on. Where do you get it? Your mom is such a little tiny thing, she's so thin I can't believe it, when she comes shopping here. Your dad must of been big, huh, you got your size from him."

"Yeah," Hugh said, turning aside to put on his apron.

"Is he dead, Hugh?" Donna asked, and there was a maternal authority to the question which he could not ignore

16

or evade but was unable to answer adequately. He shook his head.

"Divorced," Donna said, speaking the word as an ordinary one and an option certainly preferable to death; Hugh, to whose mother the word was an obscenity, unspeakable, would have agreed with relief but had to shake his head again. "Went off," he said. "I got to help Bill with the crates." And he went off. Went off, ran away, hid. Among the crates, among the imitation bacon bits and the green shifting and wink of the cash registers, anywhere, you could hide anywhere, and no place was any better than any other place.

But from time to time during the day's work he thought of the water of the creek in his mouth and on his lips. He craved to drink that water again.

He took the idea Donna had given him home with him.

"Thought I'd get up early in the morning and jog," he said at dinner. They ate on TV trays in front of the TV. "That's why I got up early this morning. To try it. Only earlier would work better, I think. Five or six, maybe. When there's no cars on the streets. And it's cool. And that way I won't bother you getting ready for work." She was beginning to glance at him warily. "If you don't mind me leaving before you do. I feel sort of out of shape. Standing around at the checkstand isn't very good exercise, I guess."

"More than you'd get sitting behind some desk all day," she said, which surprised him as a flank attack; he had not mentioned library school or anything about library work for months, since before they left the last town. Maybe she just meant office work like her own. The knife's edge was not in her voice, though it was sharp enough.

"Would it bother you if I got up and went out for a couple of hours real early? I can be back when you leave, and get my breakfast after you've gone to work."

"Why should it bother me?" she said, glancing down at her thin shoulders to arrange the straps of her summer

17

dress. She lighted a cigarette and looked at the television screen, where a reporter was describing an airplane crash. "You're perfectly free to come and go, you're twenty, nearly twenty-one years old, after all. You don't have to consult me about every little thing you want to do. I can't decide everything for you. The only thing I do insist on is not leaving the house empty at night, I did have a terrible shock night before last when I drove in and there were no lights on. It's just purely a matter of common sense and consideration for others. It has just got to the point where a person can't be safe in their own home even." She had begun to speak tightly and to flip the filter end of her cigarette repeatedly with her thumbnail. Hugh was tense, dreading the next step towards the edge; but she said no more, watching the television intently. He did not dare pursue the subject. When he went to bed nothing further had been said. Ordinarily he would have heeded the threat of hysteria and not done whatever it was he wanted to do; but in this matter he was driven. It was thirst, he must drink. He woke at five, and was standing by his bed pulling his shirt on before he was fully awake.

The apartment looked unfamiliar seen in this new light, the twilight of dawn. He did not put on his shoes till he was out on the front steps. The sun's rays ran level down the side streets from behind the apartment houses. Oak Valley Road lay in fresh blue shadow. He had no jacket, and shivered. In his haste he knotted his shoelace wrong and had to fight with the knot, like a little kid late to school; then he was off. At a jogtrot. He did not like to lie. He had said he was going jogging, so he jogged.

It took him a little less than an hour, jogging, and walking when he got out of breath, and forcing himself with increasing difficulty to jog again, to reach the woods on the far side of the waste fields. Pausing there under the eaves of the wood he checked his wristwatch. It was ten minutes to six.

Though the trees did not grow very close together the wood was a place entirely different from the open, as different as indoors from outdoors. Within a few yards the hot, bright, early sunlight was shut out except for scattered drifts and flecks of light on leaves and ground. Since leaving the suburban streets he had not seen anyone. There were no fences maintained as boundaries, though at the edge of the woods there was a straggle of rotten posts and tangled wire. More than one vague path branched off among the trees and underbrush, but he followed his way without hesitation. He noticed a fleck of tinfoil under the clawed sprays of blackberry near the path, but no beer tabs, no soft-drink cans, condoms, Kleenex, candy wrappers. Nobody came here much. The way turned left. He looked for the tall pine with the reddish, scaly trunk, and saw its upper branches dark against the sky. The path narrowed and led downward, darkening, the ground softening underfoot. He came between the pine and the high bushes, the gateway to the creek place, and there it was, the glades on the near and the far side of the water, the motion and singing of the water, and the cool air, the cool, sweet, clear twilight of late evening.

He stood on the threshold, the dark trees over him. If I look back, he thought, I'll see the sunlight through the trees. He did not look back. He went forward, walking slowly.

At the water's edge he paused to unstrap his watch. The sweep hand was not moving, the watch was stuck at two minutes to six. He shook it, then shoved it into his jeans pocket, rolled his shirt sleeves above the elbow, and knelt down on both knees. Deliberately and slowly he stooped forward, bowing down his head, setting his hands deep in the muddy sand of the verge, and drank of the running water.

A couple of yards upstream a flat boulder shelved out over the creek. He went and sat on it, leaning forward presently to put his hands in the water. Several times he ran his wet hands over his face and hair. His skin was fair, the water cold; he noticed with pleasure that his wrists and hands in the water got as red as canned salmon. The water itself was dark but clear, like smoky crystal. In sandy shallows in the lee of the boulder lay shoals of pebbles, their colors and markings intensified by the water. He watched them and the transparent curling run of the current over them, then sat up again on the shelving rock and gazed up at the colorless sky. There nothing moved. Near the black, sharp tip of a pine on the ridge across the creek he kept thinking he saw a star, from the corner of his eye, but when he looked directly for it it was not visible. For a long time he sat still, his arms clasped round his knees, over the rush and music of the water.

The chill of the breeze that crept above the creek penetrated as he sat still. He got up at last, hugging his ribs, and sauntered downstream, keeping to the bank just above the sandy edge of the stream. He looked at everything with idle, easy alertness, just tinged with caution, studying the ground, rocks, bushes and trees, the darker woods across the water. The ground was less moist and mulchy in the downstream part of the glade, where thick, coarse grass grew amongst bushes three or four feet high. The bushes were spaced apart so that the grassy areas between them were like small gardens, or roofless rooms. You could camp in one of them, Hugh thought. If you got a tent—but do you need a tent in summer? A sleeping bag would be enough. And something to cook in. And some matches. The fireplace could be down in the sand here, on the beach under the rocky dropoff of the bank. Would it be all right to light a fire here? You wouldn't actually need one unless you wanted to cook, but it would give a kind of center, a warmth . . . and then you could sleep, spend the whole night out under the sky beside the sound of the water. . . . He wandered on, making a long circuit of the clearing, stopping often to look at things and to ponder. The movements of his body here were large, slow, and free, always with that slight and rather enjoyable element of caution, because it was strange ground, the wild. Coming back at last to the shelving rock he knelt once more to drink, then stood up, went resolute to the gateway between the high bushes and the pine, glanced back once, and left the place.

The path was steep, dim, hard to follow. Branches lashed his face; he must turn his head aside, shut his eyes. He turned wrong somewhere at the top and went through a patch of woods he had not seen, a sunken, weedy region where the thin trees grew in clumps. He came out at the fields' edge by a deeper part of the ditch filled up with rubbish and dead stalks, facing the dazzle of the eastern sun, the bright spears of daylight. He rubbed his forehead, which stung where a blackberry trailer had caught it, and dug into his pocket for his watch. It was running again, and said the time was 6:08. It was later than that, of course, because it had not been running all the time he was by the creek, but still he could probably get home by eight. He set off, not jogging, for he was in no mood for pumping and gasping, but at a swift, steady walk. His mind was still in the quietness of the creek place, empty of anxieties and explanations. Alert and content, he strode along across the waste fields, up the rise, between the dreary farmhouses on the gravel road, past the tree farm to the corner of Chelsea Gardens Place and from street to street to 14067½-C Oak Valley Road. He let himself in, and there was his mother in her chintz wrapper, staring; she had just got up. The kitchen clock said it was five minutes to seven. His watch said it was four minutes to seven.

He sat down at the dinette table with a large bowl of cornflakes and two nectarines and ate, because he was hungry; the last twenty blocks he had thought mainly about breakfast. As he ate, however, his thoughts were not on breakfast. How had he spent an hour going to the creek place and an hour there and an hour coming back, between five o'clock and seven o'clock? And it was—

His mind balked. He hunched his shoulders, drew his head down, felt his chest tighten in resistance, but drove himself ahead at the words: It was evening, there, by the creek. Late evening, twilight. The stars coming out. He had got there at six in the morning in sunlight and come out at six in the morning in sunlight, and while he had been there it had been late evening. The evening of what day?

"You want a cup of coffee?" his mother asked. Her voice was creaky with sleep, but not sharp.

"Sure," Hugh said, still pondering.

He refilled his bowl with cornflakes, not wanting to cook while his mother was there, not wanting to bother with cooking anyhow. He sat, spoon in hand, brooding.

His mother set a willow-ware mug of coffee down in front of him with a little flourish. "There, your majesty!"

"Hunks," he said, breakfast-tablese for Thanks, and went on eating and staring.

"When did you go out?" She sat down across the Formica table from him with her cup of coffee.

"About five."

"You jogged all that time, two hours?"

"I don't know. Sat around some."

"You shouldn't overdo any kind of exercise in the beginning. Start slow and build it up. Two hours, that's too much to begin with. You could do things to your heart. Like when people shovel snow in the winter the first time it snows and hundreds of them drop dead in the driveway every year. You have to start slow."

"All in the same driveway?" Hugh murmured, with a vague look of awakening.

"Where did you run, anyhow? Just around and around? It must look funny."

"Oh, sort of around. Lot of empty streets." He stood up. "I'm going to make my bed and stuff," he said. He

22

yawned hugely. "Not used to getting up so early." He looked down at his mother. She was so small and thin, so tense and fierce, he wished he could pat her shoulder or kiss her hair, but she hated to be touched, and he always did it wrong anyhow.

"You haven't touched your coffee."

He looked down at the full mug; obediently drank it off in a couple of long gulps; and mooched off towards his room. "Have a good day," he said.

He would not have gone back but for the taste of the water. That water he must drink; no other quenched his thirst. Otherwise, he told himself, he would have stayed away, because there was something crazy going on. His watch would not run there. Either he was crazy or there was something unexplainable going on, some kind of monkeying with time, the kind of thing his mother and her occultist friend were interested in and he was not interested in and had no use for. Ordinary things were weird enough without getting messed up any farther, and life didn't need any more complications than it had already. But the fact was, the one place where his life did not seem complicated was the place by the creek, and he had to go back there to be quiet and think and be alone; to drink the water, to swim in the water.

On his third visit there he decided to wade. He took off his shoes. The creek looked pretty shallow. He stepped into a deep bit and got wet to mid-thigh; splashed ashore, took off jeans, shirt, shorts, returned naked to the cold, noisy water. At its deepest it came no higher than his ribs, but there was one place where he could swim a few strokes. He went under, the strong currents pushing him, his hair floating loose around his face in the strange dark clarity

23

of the underwater. He swam, scraped his knees on hidden rocks, set his hands and feet down on soft unseen surfaces, fought the shouting white water between boulders where the current raced. He came out of the water like a buffalo charging, shaking and stamping with cold and energy, and rubbed himself dry with his shirt. After that he always swam when he went there.

Since he came to the creek place only early in the morning, he kept thinking that he could not spend the night there, as he had imagined doing. And indeed he could not spend the night there, because it was never night there. It was never any different. It did not change. It was late evening. Sometimes he thought it was a little darker, or a little lighter, than last time; but he was never sure. He had never seen the star near the top of the high tree straight on, but was certain it was there in the same place each time. But his watch did not run, there. Time did not go. It was like an island, time running to either side of it like the water of a river, like the tides past a rock in the sand. You could go there and stay and you would come out to the moment you left. Or almost. When he felt he had been there an hour or longer, his watch seemed to show a few minutes had passed, when he returned to the sunlight. Maybe it did not stop, maybe it ran very slowly there, time was different there, entering the glade you entered a different time, a slower time. That was nonsense, not worth thinking about.

The fourth or fifth time he spent a long while at the creek place, swimming, making and sitting by a fire; by early afternoon, working at Sam's, he was groggy, half asleep. If he did stay and sleep at the creek place, he wouldn't have to stay awake twenty hours on end. He would live two lives. In fact he would live two lives in the space of one, twice as long in the same amount of time. He was arranging celery in the showcase when this occurred to him. He laughed, and found his hands shaking. A customer looking over the vegetables, a bony old man, glared at the mushrooms at $2.24 and said, "Crazy people taking psychologic drugs, ought to be taught a lesson." Hugh did not know whether the old man was talking about him or the mushrooms or something else altogether.

He took his lunch hour to go to the cut-rate sporting-goods store in the shopping center across the freeway. Most of his week's wages went for a bedroll, a stock of camping victuals, a good two-bladed jack-knife, and an irresistibly compact steel cooking kit. He turned back on the way to the cash register and added a cheap Army-surplus backpack. As he stuffed the food packets into the backpack he realized that he could not take it home. His mother was not going out tonight. She would be there when he came in. What's all that, Hugh, what have you got a backpack for, a *sleeping* bag, but if you get one worth getting at all they cost a lot of money, just when do you think you're going to *use* all this expensive stuff. He had been a fool to buy it all, to buy any of it. What did he think he was doing? He lugged it all through the heat back to Sam's Thrift-E-Mart, left it locked in the freezer in the back storeroom, and went to the manager to ask permission to leave work an hour early.

"What for?" the sour man said, crouching in his office that was littered with empty cardboard cans of loganberry yogurt, and smelled of old yogurt and cigars.

"My mother's sick," Hugh said.

As he said the words he turned white and sweat started out on his face.

The manager stared at him, perhaps intimidated, perhaps indifferent. After a long staring pause he said, "O.K.," and turned his back.

Hugh left the manager's office feeling the floor and walls skip and sway. The world went white and small like the white of an egg, the white of an eye. He was sick. She was sick, yes, she was sick, and needed help.

I do help her. My God, what can I do that I'm not doing? I don't go anywhere, I don't know anybody, I'm not going to school, I work close to home where she knows where I am, I'm home every night, I'm with her on weekends, everything she asks—what can I do that I don't do?

His self-accusation was, he knew, unjust, and it did not matter if it was just or unjust: it was judgment; he could not escape it. His bowels felt loose and he was still a little dizzy. He got through his work clumsily, making stupid errors over and over at the register. It was Friday, a heavy afternoon. He could not close his checkline till ten after five, and then only by getting Donna to take his place. "You sick, honey?" she asked him, as he gave her the register key. He did not dare repeat the lie lest it eat the truth again. "I don't know," he said.

"You take care now, Buck."

"I will."

He made for the back of the store, clumsy and blundering among the crowded aisles. He got his bedroll and backpack from the coldroom and set off through the streets, eastward not westward, towards the paint factory, the waste fields, the gateway. He had to get there. It would be all right when he got there. It was his place. He was all right there.

The fields were furnace hot. Soaked with sweat and his mouth dry as plaster, Hugh struggled on into the woods, left heat and bright day behind him as the path went downwards and he crossed the threshold of the dusk. He set down his load and went as always straight to the stream bank, knelt, and drank. He stripped off his sweaty clothes and walked out into the water. His breath caught in a ha! of painful ecstasy at the cold of it, the push and force and curl of the current, the grainy skin of rocks under his soles and against his palms. He slipped into the deep pool, dived under, let the water take him, the water in him, he in the water, one dark joy. All else forgotten.

He came up blinded by his hair, floated for a while under

the circle of the colorless, cloudless sky, then at last, the cold of the water striking to the bone, touched ground and splashed ashore. Always he went in silently, with reverence, and came out noisily, charged with life. He rubbed down, pulled on his jeans, and sat down beside his backpack to open it ceremonially. He would make his camp; he would cook dinner. He would lay out his bed there in the shelter of the shrubs in the high grass, and lie down, and sleep beside the running water.

He wakened under the dark trees, the odor of mint and grass in his head. The faint wind touched his face and hair like a dark, transparent hand.

It was a strange, slow wakening. He had not dreamed, yet felt that he was dreaming. Entire trust and confidence possessed him. Having lain down and slept on this ground he belonged to it. No harm would come to him. This was his country.

He got up and washed himself at the creek; kneeling on the shelving rock above the water he looked across to the pale grass of the glade on the other side, the dark masses of bushes and foliage, the clarity of sky over the trees. He stood up then, and set out across the creek, barefoot, not in the water this time but going from rock to rock till a final broad step took him onto the sand of the farther shore. Mint grew on the weedy bank above the sand on this side, too. He picked a leaf, ritually, and chewed it. Farside mint was the same as nearside mint. There was no boundary. It was all his country. But this time, this was far enough: he would go no farther now. Part of the pleasure of being here was that he could listen for and obey such impulses and commands coming from within him, undistorted by external pressures and compulsions. In that obedience, for the first time since early childhood, he sensed the headiness of freedom, the calmness of power. He chose now to go no farther. When he chose to go farther he would do so. Chewing the mint leaf he strode with wide, steady steps back across the stream.

He dressed, packed up his bedroll neatly and tucked it away well concealed in the hollow under a bush, put the knapsack with the food in it up in the fork of a tree—he had read about doing that, to keep it safe from something, bears, ants? anteaters? anyhow it seemed better than leaving it lying around—then knelt to drink from the creek once more, and left.

He got to Oak Valley Road at seven in the evening of the day he had left work at five-fifteen. His mother had not made any dinner; it was too hot to cook, she said; they went to a chain restaurant for a hamburger, and to a movie afterwards.

He thought he would be awake all night, having slept at the creek place, but he slept sound in bed, only waking earlier and easier than ever, at four-thirty, before sunrise, in the other twilight, the first, the twilight of morning. By the time he got to the woods the sun had risen in bright, tremendous splendor of summer. He turned from that, going down into the evening land, tranquil and eager, ready to cross the water and explore, to learn this realm beyond reason and beyond question, his own place, his own country. He knelt by the clear, dark water to drink. He lifted his head from the water to see where he would go, and saw facing him across the gleaming, sinuous, continual movement of the stream, on the far shore, a square sign nailed on a board stuck into the bank, black words on white, KEEP OUT—NO TRESPASSING.

2

Maybe the gate was always shut now, shut forever: gone. To go to Pincus's woods and to the place where it should be and see the stupid daylight, the dusty thickets, the culvert, finally the barbed-wire fence across the first slope of the hill, no path down, no gate, there was no use doing that over and over. The first time it had been shut, two years ago, she had stood there where it should have been and willed to open it, willed it to be open, commanded it to be. And come back the next day and the next, and crouched down and cried. Then after a week she had come back and the gate was there, and she had gone in, as easy as that. But she could not count on it. Probably it would not be there. She had not even tried for months; it was stupid to keep trying. It made her feel like a fool, like a kid playing games, playing hide and seek with nobody to play with. But the gate was there. She went through into the twilight.

She went forward squinting and suspicious, walking as if the ground might get pulled out from under her like a rug. Then she dropped down on all fours and kissed the dirt, pressing her face against it like a suckling baby. "So," she whispered, "so." She stood up and reached up at full stretch toward the sky, then went to the water's edge, knelt, washed her face and hands and arms noisily, drank, answered the water's loud, continual singing, "So you are, so I am, so." She sat down crosslegged on the shelving rock, sat still, shut her eyes to contain her joy.

It had been so long, but nothing was changed, nothing ever changed. Here was always. She should do what she always did when she was a kid, thirteen, when she first found the beginning place, before she had even crossed the river; she could do the things she used to do, the fire worship and the endless dance, the time she had buried the four stones in the place under the grey tree upriver. They would still be there. Nothing would move them here. Four stones in a square, black, blue-grey, yellow, white, and the ashes of her burnt offering, the wooden figure she had carved, in the center. That had all been silly, kid stuff. The things people did in church were silly too. There were reasons for doing them. She would dance the endless dance if she felt like it; keep it going; that was the thing about it, it didn't end. This was the place where she did what she felt like. This was the place where she was her self, her own. She was home, home— No, but on the way home, on the way at last again, now she could go, now she would go, across the triple river and on to the dark mountain, home.

She stood up on the shelf-rock, and with arms stretched out wide and hands held hollowed as if they bore bells or bowls of flame or water, danced on the rock, quick sway-ing sweeping movements, danced to the beach, to the cross-ing—and stopped short.

In a circle of stones on the sand a few yards downriver from the crossing lay the ashes of a fire.

Nearby, utensils and packets, half hidden under the drooping branches of an elder. Plastic, steel, paper.

Noiseless, she took one step forward. The ashes were still hot: she caught the tang of burning.

No one came here. No one ever. Her place alone. The gateway for her, the path for her, alone. Who, hiding, had watched her dance, and laughed? She turned, searching, rigid, to defy the enemy, "Come on, come out, then!" when, with a shock of pure fear that took all breath, she saw the pale enormous arm grope out towards her across the grass—

seeing even as she saw the monstrous reaching thing what it was, a dun-colored sleeping bag, somebody in a sleeping bag on the grass there by the bushes. But the shock had been so hard that she sank down now, squatting, rocking her body a little, till her breath came back and the whiteness left the edges of her vision. Then, cautiously, she stood up once more and peered across the bushy edge of the riverbed. She could tell only that the sleeping bag was motionless. If she took another step here she must step on soft sand and leave a footprint. She drew back to the shelf-rock, stepped up from it to the grass, and circled back behind the elder bushes till she got a clear view of the intruder. A white heavy face blanked out by sleep, jaw slack, light hair loose, the long mound of the bag like a sack of garbage, like a dog turd lying on the ground of the beloved place, the ground she had kissed, her own, the ain country.

She stood there as motionless as the sleeper. Then she turned suddenly and went quick and light, noiseless in tennis shoes, to the crossing and across in the familiar pattern of rock to rock above the merry water, up the far bank, and off on the south road; going a traveler's pace, not a run or trot but a fast, even, lightfoot walk that put the distances behind her. As she went she gazed straight ahead and for a long way, a long time there was no clear thought in her mind, only the backwash of terror and anger and, that gone, the dry emptiness she knew too well, whatever one called it, maybe it was grief.

There was nowhere, nowhere to go, nowhere to be. Even here no peace or place.

But the way she went itself said *you are going home.* Her skin touched the air of the ain country, her eyes looked

31

into the dusk forests. The rhythm of walking, of the up-slopes, the downslopes, the rivers, the long rhythms of the land quieted grief, filled emptiness at last. The farther she went into the twilight the more wholly she belonged to it, till all thought of the daylight world was gone and even the memory of the intruder at the beginning place was dulled, her mind tuned to what was about her as she walked and to the goal of her walking. The forests darkened, the way grew steep. It was a long time since she had come to Mountain Town.

And a long way. She always forgot how long, how hard. When she had first found the way she used to break the journey with a sleep at Third River, at the foot of the mountain. Since she was sixteen she had been able to get to Tembreabrezi all in one pull, but a tough one, up the steep, dark slopes and up and on, always farther than she remembered. She was footsore, legweary, and very hungry when she came at last to the clear road and the long turning. But that was the joy of it, to come there worn out, craving food and warmth and rest, glad to the heart to see the lighted windows in the cold sweep of mountainside and sky, and smell the woodsmoke of the fires, the smell that from the ancient beginnings whispers, *You are coming out of the wilderness, coming home.* And to hear the voices speak her name.

"Irena!" cried little Aduvan, in the street in front of the inn yard, startled at first, then breaking into a smile and a shout to her playmates, "Irena tialohadji!"—Irena has come back!

Irene hugged and swung the child till she squealed, and the troop of four little ones all shrieked in their sweet, thin voices to be hugged and swung, dancing about her till Palizot looked out of the courtyard to see what the commotion was, and came forward wiping her hands on her apron, calm, saying, "Come in, come in, Irena. You've come a long way, you'll be tired." So she had welcomed

Irene the first time she ever came to Mountain Town, four-teen years old, hungry, dirty, tired, frightened. She had not known the language then but she had understood what Palizot said to her: *Come in, child, come home.*

The fire was burning in the big hearth of the inn. An excellent perfume of onion, cabbage, and spices pervaded the rooms. Everything was as it had been, as it ought to be, with a couple of improvements to be admired: the floors were covered with a reddish straw matting, instead of sand scattered on the bare wood. "That's nice, it's warmer," Irene said, and Palizot, pleased but judicious, "I don't know yet how it will wear. Let's have some light in here beside the fire. Sofir! Irena has come! Will you stay a while with us, levadja?"

Child, the word meant, dear child; they added the 'adja' onto names too, making them endearments. It pleased her deeply when Palizot called her that. She nodded, having already resolved to spend twelve days here, overnight on the other side of the gate. She was trying to arrange the words for a question, and they did not come at once, for it had been months since she spoke the language. "Palizot. Tell me. Since I was here—has anyone come, on the south road?"

"No one has come on any road," Palizot said, a strange answer, her voice calm and grave. Then Sofir came up from the cellars with cobwebs in his thick black hair, a baritone man the same size from chest to hip so you could have made round sections of him like a treetrunk; he hugged Irene, shook both her hands, rumbling joyfully, "A long while, Irenadja, a long while, but you've come!"

They gave her her favorite room, and she helped Sofir carry up wood for the hearthfire there. He laid and lit the fire at once to warm and air the room, which felt as if it had not been used for a long time. There were no other guests staying at the inn. In itself that was nothing unusual, but she began to notice other indications that few travelers and little trade had been coming to the inn. The big pewter beer cans hung in a row along the wall had not been taken down and used lately, from the look of them, for a boisterous tradesmen's evening or to welcome a party of cloth buyers up from the plains. She went to see what beasts were in the inn stable, but there were none, the stalls and mangers empty. Despite Sofir's excellent cooking the food at supper was coarse, and there was none of his fine wheat bread with it, only the stiff dark porridge made of the grains they grew here on the mountain. About Sofir and Palizot there was some air of trouble or constraint, but they said nothing directly about the lack of business, and Irene found she could not ask them. With them she was "the child" still, welcomed and cherished because she had no part in their adversities and cares. So it had always been heart's holiday for her with them; and she did not know how to change that if she wanted to. As always, then, they talked of nothing important, the important thing being their love.

After supper a few townsfolk came in to spend the evening. Sofir tended bar in the big front room for the men. The women joined Palizot by the fire in the snug room off the kitchen. They drank the local beer and chatted; old Kadit knocked back a quarter pint or so of apple brandy. Irene had a very small mug of the beer, which was powerful stuff, and helped Palizot sew patchwork. She detested sewing, but this work with Palizot was an old pleasure, one of the things she thought of with yearning from the other side of the gate: the scraps of soft colored wool, the firelight and lamplight, Palizot's long, grave, mild face, the women's quiet voices and Kadit's huffing laugh, the buzz and grumble of the men talking in the other room, her own sleepiness, the stillness of the great old house overhead and the quietness of the streets of the town, of the forests beyond the streets.

When the lamps were lighted and the curtains and shutters closed it always seemed that it was night outside. She did not open the shutters of her bedroom window till she got up after the night's sleep, when the unchanging twilight looked like the dusk of a winter morning. So the townspeople spoke of it, saying morning, midday, night. Learning their language Irene had learned those words, but they did not always come unquestioned to her tongue. What meaning could they have, here? But she could not ask Palizot or Sofir, or Aduvan's mother Trijiat, or the other women she was fond of; her questions did not come clear; they laughed and said, "Morning comes before midday and evening after it, child!"—always entertained by her difficulties with the language, and ready to help her, but not to question their own certainties. There was no one in Mountain Town who might be able to speak of such matters but the Master. So she used to plan to ask him why there was no day and night here, why the sun never rose and yet you never saw the stars, how this could be. But she had never asked him a word of it. What were the words in his language for sun, for star? And if she said, "Why is it never day or night here?" it would sound stupid, since day meant waking and night meant sleeping, and they waked and worked and slept like anybody on the other side. She could begin to explain, "Where I came from there is a round fire in the sky," but it would sound like a Hollywood caveman in the first place, and in the second and larger place she never talked about where she came from. From the start, from the first time she went through the gate, the first time she crossed First River, the first time she came to Mountain Town, she had known that you did not talk of one place in the other place. You did not tell them where you came from, unless they asked. No one, in either country, ever asked.

She was convinced that the Master knew something of the existence of the gate. Perhaps he knew much more than that; though she did not admit it quite clearly to herself she believed that in fact he knew much more than she

35

did and would, when he chose, explain it all to her. But she dared not ask him. It was not yet time. She knew so little, even yet, of the ain country, except for the south road, and the town itself, the people of the town and their trades and feuds and jokes and crafts and gossip and manners, which she never tired of learning, and their language, which she could chatter away in and yet sometimes did not understand at all. Always outside the benign hearthcenter lay the twilight and the silence, the unexplained, the unexplored. She had been content that it was so. She had wished that nothing here be changed. But this time, even the first night, at the first hearthfire, she felt the circle broken. It was no longer safe. Though she might wish it, and they might wish it, she was not a child any more.

After breakfast she went for a visit with Trijiat, and then walked Aduvan and her little brother to the cobbler's, at the other end of town, to leave their mother's good shoes to be resoled. The little girl talked all the way and the little boy chirped like a cricket. Their heads were full of some ghost story or tall tale they had been told, and they kept asking Irene if she wasn't scared when she walked on the mountain. Virti ran ahead, hid behind a porch, leapt out at her making terrifying roars like a cricket gone hysterical, and she performed suitable cries of terror and dismay. "You have to fall down!" Virti said, but she declined to fall down. The errand done, she left the children with their grandmother, and turned from the town's main street to the steepest of the narrow cobbled ways going up the hillside, so steep that at intervals the street broke into steps, like a person breaking into giggles or hiccups, and then resumed its sober climb, until it had another fit of steps. At the top of it stood the wall of the garden of the manor, the arched stone gate beautiful against the clear sky. Turning to the right before she reached that gate Irene halted for a moment, and looked up at the Master's house.

A dozen gables and dormers broke dark, sharp angles

on the sky; the windows, bay and bow, many-paned, lay no two on one level, so that there was no counting the stories of the house except on the evidence of three great beams across the front. The door was massive, twelve-paneled. As she lifted the brass knocker ring and struck it on the polished disc of brass, it came into Irene's mind that she had dreamed of this door many times, on the other side.

Fimol the housekeeper, erect and imperturbable in high-necked, long-sleeved, long-skirted grey, opened the heavy door and greeted the visitor to the Master's house. Fimol never smiled, and Irene had always been in awe of her. She noticed with a sense almost of disloyalty, as she followed her, that Fimol's hair had gone white and that her stiff figure was thin, the body of a frail, aging woman. They came into the hall of the house.

This was the center of it all, this high room. Facing the long wall of paneled oak were twelve high, leaded windows looking out upon the terraced garden. The sparse furniture was carved oak, the carpets of local weave, crimson, orange, and brown, warming the room even when the candles were not lit and there was only the clear constant twilight from the windows. In each end wall was a huge stone chimney-piece, and on each of these, high over the wide hearth and the mantel, hung a portrait: a stiff, melancholy lady stared with round black eyes down the length of the room at her lord, who concealed the hand of a crippled right arm inside his coat and scowled blackly back at her.

To the right of that farther hearth, near the door to his offices, the Master stood in conversation with the stonecutter Gahiar. Seeing Irene enter with the housekeeper he stared with that black ancestral scowl; then his face changed; he turned from Gahiar and strode down the long room to her, his hands held out. "Irena! You have come!"—such welcome as she had imagined from him, in daydream, often, but not in expectation, and not wondering what came next.

The Master or mayor of Tembreabrezi was a spare, swarthy man with a hawk nose and dark eyes. He wore black, rusty, neatly-mended, homespun black trousers, vest, and jacket. A harsh man, a dark man. She had loved him since she first saw his face.

He brought her out of the hall into his offices, where a fire burned and the curtains were drawn as if against the grey of a day of winter. He set her a chair, and aided by the dignity of her clothing, the dark-red skirt and homespun blouse that Palizot kept for her, she sat down without awkwardness. He stood beside the high desk where he worked standing—he was a man one seldom saw sitting down—and turned his intense look on her. She drew a deep breath and held herself quiet, her hands in her lap.

"It has been a long time, Irena."

"I could not come."

"The way—?"

"I could not—find—" Nor could she find the words she needed. "The place," she said, and then remembering what they called the stone arch in the wall of the manor, "The gateway. It was shut."

"You could not walk on the road," he said, not impatient with her stumbling, but dauntingly intent.

"When I—when I could come to the road, I could walk on it. But at the beginning—" She stuck again.

"You were afraid."

His voice was gentle; she had never heard him speak so gently.

"When I came through the gateway. It had been so long. And there, at the beginning place, beside the river, there was—"

He said a word, almost in a whisper. It was the word little Virti had shouted when he was playing monster and she would not fall down, and Aduvan had scolded him, Shut up, don't say that, both children over-excited, near

38

tears. A huge, pale, deformed arm groping out across the grass—

"A man," she said. "A stranger."

The Master listened, intent, alert.

"A stranger, like me. Not like me, but—" She knew no other way to say it. The Master, evidently understanding, nodded once.

"Did you speak with him?"

"No. He was asleep. I came on. I didn't want—I was afraid—" She stuck again. She could not explain her first panic. Surely he would see why a woman alone might have reason to be afraid of a strange man. But she could not express the rage she felt now recalling her fear and recalling the stranger, the gross sleeper, the litter of plastic trash: the sense of desecration and of danger. She clasped her hands hard in her lap and struggled again for the words she wanted, forcing herself to speak. "If he found the gateway, maybe others will find it. There are—there are so many, many people there—"

If the Master understood what she meant by "there," his only response was a black frown.

"You must guard your walls, Master!" she said desperately. She would have said "borders" but knew no such word in his language, nor any word for boundary or fence but the word that meant a wall of wood or stone.

He nodded. But he said, "There are no walls, Irena. And now, for us, no ways."

The tone of his voice held her silent. He turned to his desk and went on presently with the same forced quietness, "We can't go on the roads. They are closed. You know that some have been closed to us for a long time. The south road, your road—you know that we don't use that." She had not known it, and stared uncomprehending. "But we had the summer pastures and the High Step, and all the eastern ways, and the north road. Now we have none of

39

them. Nobody comes from Three Fountains, or the foothill villages. No traders or merchants. Nothing from the plains. No news from the City of the King. For a while we could go westward, up the mountain, on the paths; but not now. All the gates of Tembreabrezi are locked."

There were no gates to lock. Only the street that led out to the south road and the north road, and the paths up and down the mountain west and east, all open, without gate or barrier.

"Is it the King that says you cannot use the roads?" Irene asked, in frustration at not understanding, and then was alarmed at her rashness in questioning the Master. Learning his language had not, after all, been like learning Spanish in high school, *la casa* the house, *el rey* the king. . . . The word *rediai*, which she thought meant king, did not necessarily mean king, or what she meant by king; she had no way to know what it meant except by hearing it used, and it was not used often, except when they spoke of the City of the King. Perhaps it was her year of Spanish and the beginning syllable "re" that had made her decide that the word meant king. She had no way to be sure. She was afraid she had said something stupid, sacrilegious. The Master's dark face was turned away from her. She saw that his hands were clenched before him on the desk.

He had perhaps not even heard her question. "This stranger," he said, turning but not looking at her, his voice very low but harsh. And he too hesitated.

"It could be—a mistake—he mistook the way—" A tramp, she wanted to say, a wanderer, a blunderer, camping there overnight without noticing anything about the place, maybe for him there was nothing special about the place, maybe he had crossed no threshold, and he would go on the next day, hitchhiking on into the city probably, he was gone already, he did not belong here. She wanted to say all this, though she could not. She was sure now it was true. It was the truth she wanted and, she saw, that the

Master also wanted, for he understood her and considered the possibility with evident relief. He was perhaps not convinced, but she had given him some hope he wanted. He looked directly at her at last, and smiled. His smile was rare, very brief and sweet. "I did not dare hope you would come back, Irena," he said softly. If she had spoken all she could have said was, "I have always loved you," but she could not, and there was no need to. He knew his power. He was the Master.

"Will you stay with us?" he asked.

Did he mean for good? His tone was restrained; she was not sure what he meant.

"As long as I can. But I must go back."

He nodded.

"And then when I try to come back, if the gate is shut again—"

"It will open for you, I think."

His eyes were strange, dark as caverns; nothing he said changed that inward gaze.

"But why—"

"Why? When you know the answer there's no question, when there's no answer there never was a question." It sounded like a proverb, and his voice was dry and a little mocking; that was the way he had used to talk to her; his return to it comforted her.

"That is your road," he said.

He turned to his desk again, adding, almost indifferently, "The south road and the north."

"Could I go north? If something is wrong— Could I go ask for help—carry a message—?"

"I do not know," he said, only glancing at her; but there was a flicker of praise or triumph on his face, and it was that that stayed with her, after he had taken her, in accordance with the sedate ways of the house, to greet his mother and have a little formal collation and conversation with her, and after she had left the house and returned to spend the day with Trijiat. For the first time, she thought, he wanted something of her. There was something she could give him, if she could find what it was. She had come closest to it when she spoke of going north. He had turned their talk away from that at once, but not before she had seen the flicker of pleasure, of praise.

If only she could understand him better! She must take seriously what he had said half-mockingly about questions and answers: He, and she, and all of them here, were subject to the laws of the place, laws as absolute as the law of gravity, as impossible to disobey and as difficult to explain. He had told her, if she understood him at all, that none of the townsfolk could leave the town, prevented by some power or law. But it was possible that she, since she could come to Tembreabrezi, might be able to leave it. Or perhaps he had meant that, being from outside this land, she was outside its laws, and need not obey? Was that what he had meant? But she would obey him. He was her law. If she could please him: if she could find what he wanted! If he would ask, so that she could give . . .

This was the longest she had ever stayed in Mountain Town. In the old days her visits had been frequent but short; now that she could spend a week or a fortnight (a night or weekend, on the other side of the gate) if she chose to, the gate had mostly been closed to her. All her longing had been to find it open, to come through. Now she was here, settled in, living at the inn and working with Sofir and Palizot as always, visiting with her friends, playing with their children. All, as always, sat her down to table if they were eating, put her to work if they were working, made her at once and entirely at home. That had been the bliss of the old days, and was still a pleasure. But it was no longer enough. It seemed to her, now, that there was an element of falseness in it, of pretense. The peace she felt here, the homeliness, was truly theirs; but not hers. She came and would leave again, no true part of their life.

They did not need her help in their work. They did not need her.

Unless, as the Master had suggested—or had he?—she could help them not by coming here, not by being here, but by going on farther.

No one but he had yet spoken of there being anything wrong, so that at first she thought little about it. Then, as she noticed that in fact no one came to the town, and no one left the town, that they were taking the flocks only to the nearer pastures, that there were shortages of salt, of wheat flour, that when Trijiat lost her good sewing needle she was upset and looked for it for days . . . as she noticed this and that and the other thing she realised that what the Master had said was true: all the roads were closed. But why? by whom, by what? She tried once or twice to speak of the matter, with Trijiat, with Sofir; they avoided answering, Sofir with a meaningless laugh, Trijiat with such open fear that Irene knew she could not bring the subject up again. It was a taboo, or a dread so deep they could not speak of it at all. They spoke of nothing but the day's doings, and pretended that nothing was wrong. And that was the falseness she felt, the discomfort. They did need help, but they would not admit it.

What would it be like to go on from Tembreabrezi, northward, down to the plains?

A couple of years ago, a long Sunday on the other side, she had gone with Sofir and old Hobim the merchant and his crew and a train of tiny donkeys laden with woven goods, first to a village a day's walk north over the shoulder of the mountain, and then on to the town called Three Fountains, in the northeastern foothills; they had stayed there two days to trade and then come back, six days' journey altogether. She remembered where the road to Three Fountains turned off eastward and the north road went straight on towards a dark pass. How far down from there to the plains? How far across the plains to the City they spoke of? She had no idea; many days' walking, no doubt; but she could take food, and there would surely be villages or towns along the way, and so she could cross the long, twilit plains and come to the City and ask help for Tembrea-brezi. If they would send help. Or was she forbidden to go on the roads too? But they had no right to forbid her. If the Master asked her to go, she would go.

He did not send for her. She grew impatient and restless. She could not understand her friends here going about their work and never talking about what was wrong, like people with cancer saying, "I'm fine, I'm fine," like her own mother always saying, "Everything is all right," she did not want to think about that here, she resented having to think about it. Why didn't they talk about it? Why didn't they *do* something? What were they waiting for?

At last the Master sent for her to come to a gathering at his house. She had been asked to such gatherings before. Business was largely carried on at the inn, in the public room, but decisions involving more than trade were taken during unhurried, long-drawn-out, chin-rubbing conversations in the hall of the two hearths. Both men and women came; and not always, but often, the Lord of the Manor; and any visitors from other towns who were people of substance or manners. The Master's mother, Dremornet, white-haired and dark-eyed, sat in state in a velvet armchair under the portrait of the ancestor with a withered arm. If there were not many guests, most gathered about her, leaving the other hearth for private conversations; when there were more people, a group formed at each end of the room. This evening a quiet circle of women and several young men had drawn about the velvet armchair, while three or four elderly men pontificated at the Master at the other hearth. There were of course no strangers there this night but Irene. She stayed in the party with the Master's mother until he came by, signaling both of them with a glance. Lord Horn had come.

44

Dremornet gathered up her skirts and rose to greet the visitor, making him a full curtsy, after which the other women bobbed at him. Lord Horn was a thin, stiff, grey man. He made a brief, stiff bow. Not even the spectacle of the tiny, self-important old lady performing a superbly self-important curtsy uncreased the cold folds of his face. His daughter, a pace behind him, blonde, dressed in pale silks, bowed and smiled palely, and they passed on. Their function, Irene thought, was to be bowed to and to bow; they were figurehead people, empty titles. The master of the town was the one called Master, Dou Sark. But they were old-fashioned people here and kept to old ways and habits, and so they thought they had to have a lord.

The Master had glanced at her again in passing, and she soon followed him. At the second hearth the townsmen, who had been croaking away like a pond of bullfrogs, now stood solemnly about. Lord Horn listened without expression and to all appearances without interest to something the Master was telling him. The daughter had sat down, characteristically selecting the only uncomfortable chair in the room, a stiff, spindly piece covered in faded brocade. She sat bolt upright and motionless. Between her pastel insipidity and Horn's dull coldness, the Master's face was bright and dark as the embers of the fire.

"The Master tells me," Lord Horn said to Irene, and paused, looking down at her as if from a distance, from a tower several miles off, with bleared windows through which it was hard to see clearly—"Sark tells me that you met another traveler, on the south road."

"I saw a man. I did not speak to him."

"Why," said Lord Horn, and paused again while he got his slow, cold words together—"why did you not speak to him?"

"He was asleep. He was—he did not belong here—" Her need for words was hot and hasty, she grabbed at the nearest one: "He was a thief."

45

Another long pause, hard to endure. Lord Horn's grey eyes, which had put her in mind of tower windows, did not look at her any longer; but he spoke again. "How did you know that?"

"Everything about him," she said, and hearing the defensive rudeness of her tone she grew angry with the same sudden vindictive rage she had felt seeing the intruder and whenever she thought of him. What right did this old man have to ask her questions? Lordship, the hell with his lordship, another of the thousand words for bully.

"You think then that the man was not . . ." a long silence, as if Horn had run permanently out of words, ". . . could not be the one, the man who . . ."

"I do not understand."

"The man for whom we wait," Horn said.

She saw then that all of them standing there by the fireplace were watching her, and that their faces, the worn, heavy faces of middle-aged and elderly men, were intent, pleading—pleading for the right answer, the word of hope.

She looked to the Master for help, to tell her what she should say. His face was set, unreadable. Did he, all but imperceptibly, shake his head?

"The man for whom you wait," she repeated. "I do not understand. What are you waiting for? Why wait? I can go." She glanced again at the Master; his eyes were on her now, his expression though still guarded was warm; she was saying what he wanted. "If none of you can go on the roads, send me. I can carry a message. Perhaps I can bring help. Why must you wait for someone else? I am here now. I can go to the City—"

She looked from the Master to Lord Horn, and was checked by the old man's expression.

"It is a long way to the City," he said in his slow, quiet voice. "A longer journey than you know. But your courage is beyond praise. I thank you, Irena."

She stood confused, all the wind out of her sails, till

the Master, frowning, drew her away, and she understood that her interview with the Lord of the Mountain was over.

Alone in her room, early, before her departure, she opened the shutters and watched the dreaming twilight over the roofs and chimneys of the town. She was still warm from bed, she wanted to sleep longer, she wanted to stay longer. When she left would the gate close again? When would she be able, would she ever be able, to come back? The reason why she must go was remote, meaningless: She had been gone a whole night now and if she did not get back to the apartment by seven in the morning she would be late to work. . . . Work, apartment, night, morning, none of it made sense here, words without meaning. Yet, like the force or fear that kept the townspeople from leaving their town, senseless as it might be it must be obeyed. As they must not go, so she must.

As always, Palizot and Sofir were up to breakfast with her before she left, and Sofir had a packet of bread and cheese for her to take on the long walk back to the gate. They were troubled, and unable to hide their trouble. They were, she saw, afraid for her.

She looked back once as the way turned. The windows of the town glimmered faint gold in the dark sweep of the forests to the valley floor. Northward above the mountain shoulder she saw one bright star shine clear, gone the next instant, lost, like the reflection in a raindrop or the glitter of mica in sand.

After crossing the Middle River she ate Sofir's bread and cheese, and drank the aching-cold water of the river; rested a while and would have liked to fall asleep, but did not, could not; and went on. Nothing threatened her in the forest, nothing frightened her, but she could not rest. She must keep on. She held her light, fast pace, and came at last to the last rise, the crest between red-trunked firs, down the long slope to the rhododendron thickets and through them to the beginning place, the gateway clearing—and saw, before she crossed the water, the blackened ring of stones, the plastic sack half hidden under ferns, the ugly rubbish of the intruder's camp.

She drew back at once to the thickets and from their shelter watched for some while. There was no sign of the man himself. Her heartbeat slowed, her face began to burn and her ears to sing a little. She crossed the river, went to the hearth ring—cold—and kicked it apart stone by stone, kicking the stones into the water. She picked up the plastic sack and the bedroll and turned to the river; then, whispering under her breath, "Out, get out, clear out," she lugged the stuff through the gateway, up the path, and dumped it in the middle of Pincus's woods at the foot of a blackberry thicket, just off the path. Hurrying on to the edge of the woods she picked out of the ditch a board nailed to a post, the NO HUNTING sign long torn or rotted away, which her eyes if not her mind had noted twelve days (or hours) ago when she came this way. With it she returned at a run to the threshold. Only when she was across it did she think, "What if I couldn't have got through?"—but without any thrill of retrospective alarm. She was too angry for fear. She snatched a lump of charred wood from the ruined hearthplace, crossed the river, and sat down on a boulder with the signboard on her knees. Carefully, in black block letters on the ribbed, rain-bleached wood, she printed: KEEP OUT—NO TRESPASSING.

She planted the sign on the crest of the bank, where it would dominate the whole clearing to the eyes of anyone coming through the gateway. The foot of the post went into the sandy soil easily enough, but the whole thing tended to slant, and she was fetching a rock to pound it in solid when some movement across the water caught her eye. She froze, looking up over the glimmering rush of the river. The man, coming down from the threshold, straight at her. Nothing between them but the water.

He knelt down, there on the far bank, and put his head down to the water to drink. Only then did she understand that he had not seen her.

She was near enough to the great rhododendron bushes that she could crouch and draw back, all in one long pulling motion, till the white of her shirt and face was concealed by leaf and shadow. When she looked for the man again he was standing up there across the river, staring—staring at the sign, of course, her sign, KEEP OUT! Her heart leapt again and her mouth opened in a soundless, gasping laugh.

Standing up he was big, heavy-bodied, as he had looked in the sleeping bag. When he moved at last he was heavy-footed, turning to plod back up the bank. He stopped to stare at the places where his hearth, his pack, his bedroll had been. He moved, stopped, stared. Finally he turned slowly, turned his back and headed for the gateway between the laurels and the pine. Irene clenched her hands in triumph. He stopped again. He turned, and came back, straight down and across the water in a heavy, stumbling charge that brought him up the bank in a rush. He pulled up the sign, broke the board off the post, broke the board across his thigh, the charcoal smearing off on his wet hands, threw down the pieces, and looked around. "You bastards!" he said in a thick voice. "You sneaking bastards!"

"Same to you," Irene's voice said, and her legs stood up under her.

At once he turned and was coming at her. She stood her ground because her legs refused to go anywhere. "Get out," she said. "Clear out. This is private property."

The staring eyes steadied and fixed on her. He stopped. He was massive. The staring face was white and blank, mindless. The mouth said words she did not understand.

He came towards her again. She heard her own voice

49

but had no idea what it said. She was still holding the rock she had picked up. She would try to kill him if he touched her.

"You don't have to," he said in a strained, husky voice, a boy's voice. He had stopped. He turned away from her now and went back, clumsily crossing the water, up the bank, across the clearing, to the threshold.

She stood without moving and watched him.

He passed between the pine and laurels and went on. It was strange; had she never looked through the gateway from this side? The path that went up so steep and dark into the daylight looked level and open, from here across the water; it looked no different from the paths of the twilight land. She could see along it for a long way in the dusk under the trees, and could see the man walking down it, still walking away under the trees in the grey unchanging light.

3

He broke the signboard, stamped the pieces into the mud, and stood there in his shirt and jeans soaked from his stumble in the creek, his shoes full of water. "You bastards," he said, the first words he had ever spoken aloud in the twilight place. "You sneaking bastards!"

The high bushes crashed and writhed. Somebody came out of hiding there, a boy, black-haired, staring. "Get out," the boy said. "Clear out. This is private property."

"All right. Where's my stuff?" Hugh took a step forward. "It cost a week's pay. What did you do with it?"

"It's up there in the woods. Don't bring it back. Don't come back. Just get out!"

The boy stepped forward, self-righteous, jeering, hateful. Hugh could not keep himself from shaking. "All right," he said, "you didn't have to—" It was no use. He turned, plunged back down the bank and across the stream, slipping and catching himself on boulders as he crossed. He made for the gateway. He had to get out. He would get out and go, never come back, it was ruined. His stuff was up in the woods, he would go through the gate and get his stuff and never come back.

But he had already gone through the gate.

When he looked back he saw the twilight behind him and the rush of the water and the rocks breaking it, and ahead of him he saw the twilight and the path going on among the trees.

He had lost his way. There was no way.

He went on a few steps, then stopped; he stood there; then came back, passing between the high bushes and the red-barked pine, to the beginning place.

The other, the stranger, was still standing on the far bank. Not a boy but a woman, jeans and white shirt, blur of black hair, white face staring.

"I can't get out," Hugh said. "There isn't any way."

The loud sweet voices of the water ran between them.

He was very deeply frightened. He said, "If you know this place, if you live here, tell me how to get out!"

The woman came forward abruptly, crossed the creek, going light and lithe from stone to stone. She stopped by the shelving rock and pointed to the gateway. "There."

He shook his head.

"That's the gate."

"I know."

"Go on!"

"It's changed," he said. He turned and crossed the glade, went between the bushes and the pine, and went on. There was no darkening of the way, no steep scramble under shrubs and blackberry, no sunlight ahead. The trees stood close and dim in the windless dusk and there was no sound but the music of the creek behind him. He turned at last and saw the figure by the water watching him.

He came back. She came across the grass to meet him.

"It goes on," she said in a whisper. "I never saw that. It's never been closed on this side.—Come on!" She passed him, quick, rageful, going towards the gate. He came with her. The rough reddish trunk of the pine brushed his shoulder. On the dark path a bramble caught at his hair. He could scarcely see her scrambling ahead. A bird chip-chipped dryly overhead. The air smelled of smoke, rubber, gasoline, sunwarmed pine needles. The path underfoot was dry.

"There's your stuff," the woman said. His pack and bedroll lay in the scruffy grass by the thickets.

He looked at them, as if to check that everything was there. He did not dare look back. He was afraid that if he looked back the twilight would rise and come with him. The woman, the girl, his age, stood on the path, black hair, black eyes, white face.

"What place is that?" he asked her. "Do you know?"

She did not answer at once, and he thought she was not going to. "If you belonged there, you'd know," she said in her harsh, thin voice.

"I need—" He could not get the words out. Why did he stand here letting her shame him? His face was hot and stiff, had he been crying? He rubbed his jaw with his hand, hiding his mouth, to hide his shame.

"It isn't a boy scout camp," she said. "It's not for bringing all your crap into and camping and— It isn't any state park. You don't know anything about it. You don't know the rules. You don't speak the language, you don't know their— It isn't your place. You don't belong. It isn't safe."

No anger would rise to relieve him of shame. He had to stand there and take what she said, and then repeat the only thing he had to say, "I need to come back." His voice was a mumble. "I won't leave stuff there."

She shook with rage like a bit of newspaper shaken by the wind, a bit of blazing paper in a fire.

"I warn you!"

What she had said before was getting through to him. "There are—people that live there?"

After a long pause she said, "Yes. There are."

Her eyes flashed queerly in the restless light.

"They're waiting for you," she said in her stifled, jeering voice, and then came forward suddenly and passed him, not going back, as he had expected, down the path into the evening land, but passing him, abrupt, swift, solid, and going forward into the morning. Within a few feet the bulk of the thickets hid her, another moment and the slight sound of her steps was gone.

Hugh stood bewildered and bereft in the warm, slightly dusty air of the woods, which was continually shaken by the vibration of distant engines on the ground and in the air. A spot of sunlight filtering in through leaves danced on the dun cover of his bedroll, in constant motion.

Where do I go now? There isn't anywhere to go.

He was tired, worn out by emotions—anger, fear, grief. He sat down there beside the path, one hand on his backpack, protectively, or for reassurance. The dreary ache of loss would not leave him or grow less.

Maybe she feels like this too, he thought. Like I took it away from her.

But I can't help it. I have to go back. I don't have anywhere else. She has no right. . . . That was not the appropriate word, but he did not know how else to put it.

I will go back. I won't leave my stuff there. Not at the gateway clearing, anyhow. I could go farther—up the creek a ways. She can't go everywhere. There's no reason we'd ever have to see each other.

Unless I can't get out again.

That thought went through his mind quite lightly. The panic terror he had submitted to when the gateway led only farther into the twilight had already sunk down deep in him, too deep to stir up easily. If it's like that again I can wait, he told himself, and go through with her when she comes.

She's like me, she comes from here. But there are people who live there, she said.

But his mind slipped away from this idea too. I don't have to meet them. There's never been anybody at the creek place. And she's gone now. I'm going back. . . .

He shoved his gear under the dusty, spiny outskirts of the thicket, stood up, and went back down the path to the threshold and into the twilight, to the clear water where, at last, he knelt and drank. The water washed his face and his hands, washed away shame and fear. "This is my home," he said to the earth and rocks and trees, and with his lips almost on the water, whispered, "I am you. I am you."

He got to Sam's Thrift-E-Mart at ten and by ten-five was opening up Line Seven. Donna looked over from the register in Six. "You O.K., Buck?"

For Hugh two days and three nights had passed since he left work an hour early yesterday afternoon; he did not remember why Donna might think he wasn't O.K. "Sure!" he said.

She looked him up and down with a curious expression, cynical yet admiring. "You wasn't sick at all," she said. "You had something better to do." She rang up a sixpack of cola and a packet of cocktail cheese snacks for a shaky, unshaven old man, remarking to him and to Hugh, "Ain't it wonderful to be young? But I wouldn't go through it again if you paid me."

He did not explore far downstream. The gorge of the creek deepened; it always seemed darker in that direction. Upstream from the gateway clearing there was less under-brush, and in many places the creek had clear, broad, sandy verges. He came to a place where the creek, under a stand of big willows, was narrowed by an outcropping of red rock that slanted across the streambed in steps and shelves. Above the white water lay a deep, long pool. The shores were overhung by trees, but the pool itself lay open to the sky. The place had about it a sense of remoteness, self-containment; no one else would come here.

He made a cache for his gear, the fork of a low tree, so thickly overgrown with a small-leafed vine that it was hidden even from him till he put his hands on it. He gathered a little supply of firewood, mostly branches from a dead tree nearby, and scooped a fireplace in the sand of the sheltered bank just above the barrier of red rocks. He laid a fire ready. Then he took off his shirt and jeans and silently, holding his body straight, walked out into the still pool. Just above the rock barrier it was deeper than he was tall. There he swam in silent and intense delight until he could bear the cold no longer, and made for the shore cramped and shuddering, and lighted his fire.

The flames were beautiful in the clear twilight. He crouched naked to get the heat on his skin, in his bones. At last he dressed, and made himself a cup of the sweet coffee-chocolate mix he had bought on sale, and sat drinking it in peace of heart. When the fire had burned down he covered all trace of it with sand, put on his shoes, and set off to explore farther upstream.

He came daily now. Half his life was spent in the twilight land. When he was there even the rhythm of his breathing was different; was deeper. When he woke from the sleep he slept there, a sleep deeper than dream, dark and resistless as the currents of the stream, he would lie a while, lazy, listening to the water run and the leaves stir, thinking, I'll stay here . . . I'll stay another while. . . . He never did. When he was at work in the supermarket, or at home, he did not think much about the evening land. It was there, that was all he had to know while he was checking out a sixty-dollar load of groceries or getting his mother quieted down after a rough day at the loan company where she worked. It was there, and he could come back to it, the silence that gave words meaning, the center that gave the world a shape.

He had never found the gate closed again, and had given

the possibility very little thought. It had had something to do with the girl. It had happened because of her, because of her being there, and that was why she had been able to unhappen it, going with him through to the other side. From time to time he thought about her, apprehensive yet regretful. If she had not been so full of hate and spite maybe they could have talked. He had let her push him around, it was his fault. She might have told him something about this land. Apparently she had known it longer and knew it better than he did. If she didn't live here, she knew those who did.

If there were any others. He thought about that a good deal, during his silent whiles at the willow place. All she had said was something like, "You don't know the language," and then when he had asked if there were people living here she had said yes, but after hesitating, and with something faked or forced in what she said. She had been trying to scare him. And the idea was threatening. It was being alone here that was the joy of it. Being alone, not having to try to handle other people, their needs, demands, commands.

But people who lived here, what could they be like? What language would they speak? Nothing here spoke. No bird ever sang. There must be animals in the woods but they were elusive, silent. There was no need for anybody here to bother anybody else.

He thought about these things when he sat in the silence by the bright small fire beside the water under the willows. A thought here could occupy his mind for a long time, having room to expand and think itself through. He had never felt himself to be particularly stupid, and had done well enough in school in the subjects he liked, but he knew people found him stupid because he had no quickness. His mind would not work in a hurry, would not rush. Here he could come and think things out, and that made a great part of the freedom he felt here. The alternation of two utterly different lives, the repeated crossing of the threshold between Kensington Heights and the evening land, might have confused and exhausted him, if it had not been for the strength he got from his whiles by the creek. He was quiet, occupied simply and fully with hiking, swimming, sleeping, thinking, using his senses; and that full quietness replaced all the sense of being pushed and hurried through life without time to ask what he was doing or where he ought to go, without time to see that there were choices, and to choose. Even there, if he held fast to the quietness he found here, even there he managed to get some thinking done.

Since he had said his mother was sick, had heard his voice say the word, he had been self-compelled to face the idea instead of running and hiding from it; to try to consider steadily how sick she was, and what her sickness was.

That was hard. It meant comparing: as if she was not his mother, but any woman, anyone. Anyone sick.

In his last couple of high schools he had known fellows who went the hard-drug route, all the way. And in tenth grade, it was not a memory he wanted to dig up, the girl who used to copy his English assignments sometimes, he could not think of her name—she always made him feel guilty because she was so humble—Cheryl was her name, and one day the week before school was out she had locked herself in a stall in the girls' room and tried to stuff herself down a toilet. He had heard the screaming and seen a girl in the hall laughing in a horrible whooping way, and then Cheryl carried out doubled up, with pinkish water dripping out of her hair, screaming in a high thin voice, and he and all the other kids standing watching, people running up the stairs to see. Nobody had known how to talk about it afterwards, nobody who had heard the screaming. That was the worst he had been close to so far, but working in groceries you saw a lot of people scolding the mushrooms, and crazies like the shoplifter who tried to bribe his way out or the guy who pulled a knife on Donna when she refused to cash his check without ID; and people doing things that might have a reason but looked pretty weird, such as buying forty-eight bottles of germkiller spray and a can of water chestnuts. What all these people had in common, as well as he could figure it out, was a kind of getting out of gear, out of synch. The engine made a noise but no power got to the wheels. They were stuck. They got nowhere. In the last seven years his mother had changed houses thirteen times and lived in five different states; and the oftener she moves, he thought, the more she doesn't get anywhere.

All the same, even if she was like the mushroom people and the germ-spray people, she wasn't as bad as the junkies or Cheryl. She was stuck but not sunk. The loan company, a huge outfit with offices all over the country, had let her transfer twice now, and still gave her raises. She complained a lot about the work, but never missed a day at it. And in this office she had made a friend finally, Durbina, and found a whole new interest, this previous-lives business, which she was getting very deep into. Was that crazy? Hugh had no inclination to judge it one way or the other. What she told him sounded pretty silly. They always seemed to remember being princesses or high priestesses in their previous lives; he wondered who had worked at the loan companies and the supermarkets in Ancient Egypt. But then, no doubt you tended to remember the high points. It was screwy, but no screwier than most things people got interested in: baseball scores, aluminum futures, antique medicine bottles, nuclear proliferation, Jesus, politics, health foods, playing the violin. People did very strange things. People were extremely strange. All of them. You couldn't judge sickness by strangeness, or everybody would come out sick. Sick was when you drove the car in neutral. The place she couldn't get away from was home, the more she left it the worse she was stuck; could not bear to be alone in the house, could not come home at night to an empty house, lived in terror of waking up at night with no one else there. And that had got worse. She was worse now than she had ever been— But I know that, he thought. What's the good of knowing it? There's nothing I can do. She hasn't got anybody but me. You have to have some-body, even if neither of you can do anything. There isn't anybody else. He

was waiting for Hugh at the corner across from school. "Let's go watch the track events down at the college practice field," he said, and Hugh, thirteen, wearing the green shirt he had got yesterday for his birthday, noticed the other kids noticing his dad, a big, fair man, tall and broad-chested, looking good in a jeans jacket gone white at the seams. He had the Ford truck there and they drove down to the college track and watched runners, broad jumpers, pole vaulters in the golden haze of the April afternoon. They talked about the last Olympics, about the techniques of pole vaulting. His dad punched his shoulder gently and said, "You know, Hughie, I have a lot of confidence in you. You know that? I can count on you. You're steadier than a lot of grown men I know. You keep that way. Your mom's got to have somebody to depend on. She can depend on you. It means a lot to me, knowing that." Hugh could not kiss the large, gold-haired hand; the only way men were allowed to touch each other was by hitting. He could not even touch the frayed cuff of the jeans jacket. He sat silent in the sudden blissful sunlight of praise. Next day when he got home from school their neighbor Joanna was there, thin-lipped, in the kitchen; Hugh's mother was lying down, under sedation; his father had gone off in the Ford truck leaving a note saying he had a job in Canada and thought this was a good time to make the break.

Hugh never saw the note, though Joanna had repeated a couple of phrases from it, such as "a good time to make the break," and he knew his mother kept it among her papers and photographs in a file box.

He had got lousy grades the rest of that term, because his mother had kept him out of school by any means she had, usually by having a crying jag at breakfast. "I'll come back, I'm just going to school. I'll be back at three-thirty," he would promise. She would cry and beg him to stay with her. When he did stay he did not know what to do with himself but read old comic books; he was afraid to go out and afraid to answer the telephone in case it was the school attendance officer calling; his mother never seemed to be glad to have him there. That summer they had moved for the first time, and she had got a job. Things were always better for a while at first in the new places.

Once she had started working she could cope with daytime all right, and he finished school without any problem. It was the night, the darkness, that she still couldn't handle, being alone in the dark. So long as she knew he was there she was all right. Who else did she have to depend on?

And what else did he have but his dependability? Anything else he might have thought he was or was worth his father had pretty well devalued by leaving. People don't leave necessary things, or valuable things. But though he understood well enough what Cheryl had felt like, like shit, that ought to be got rid of, he wasn't going to do anything about it, as Cheryl had tried to do, because in one respect he was valuable, useful, even necessary: he could be there when his mother needed somebody to be there. He could take his father's place. Sort of.

When he had to go out for track in spring in tenth grade,

he broke his ankle pole vaulting the first day. He was never any good at sports. He got big and tall, but heavy, with soft muscles, soft skin.

"Hey, I'm going to get one of those cute red suits and start running up and down the street too," Donna said. "Where's your spare tire gone to, Buck?" He looked down at his belly self-consciously but saw that maybe it did look better than it used to. No wonder, since every morning before work he got in a long fast walk plus something like ten or twelve hours of hiking and swimming and not eating very much. Getting enough food into the evening land was a problem which he solved mainly by going hungry there.

His first explorations farther upstream had been tentative and short. He was afraid of getting lost. He bought a compass and then discovered he did not know how to use it. The needle flittered and veered at every step, and though it seemed most of the time to indicate that north was across the creek (if north was the blue end of the needle) he would need a bit more than that to get back to the gateway clearing if he got deep into the hills upstream. There were no stars or sun to take directions from. What did north mean, here? The trees grew close enough that walking could never be straight for very long, and he found no open viewpoint, no way to get an idea of the lay of the land. So he explored the paths and thickets, hollows, glades, side valleys, hillside springs, windings and turnings of the forest on both sides of the creek upstream from the willow place. He learned that piece of wilderness. He had a lot to learn. He knew nothing about wilderness, woodcraft, plants. Trees with cones were pines. Trees with drooping stringy branches were willows. He knew oaks, there had been a huge oak on the playground of one of his high schools, but none of the trees in this forest looked like it. He got a book on common trees and succeeded in identifying several: ash, maple, vine maple, alder, fir. Everything he saw and all that came under his hand interested and occupied him, here. He thought also about what he did not know and had not seen. How far did the wilderness, the forest, go on? Was there any end to it? He had gone several miles now along the creek and there was no change, no slightest track or sign of mankind. Even the birds and beasts were all but unseen; he followed the faint paths of the deer but never saw one, found sometimes an old bird's nest fallen, but never, in the changeless time and season and the weather without change, heard an animal cry out, or a bird sing.

The creek, his companion and his guide: what of it? It must join a river, or become a river, downstream, and large or small it must run at last into the sea.

His breath caught. He stared blankly at his fire, his mind held by that thought: the sea that lay beyond the coasts of evening. The darkness to which this living water ran. White breakers in the last of dusk and out beyond them the depths, the night. The night, and all the stars.

So vast and dark was that vision, so terrible the thought of the stars, that when it left him and he looked around again at the familiar rocks, sandbars, trees, branches, leaf patterns of his camping place, everything seemed small and fragile, toylike, and the flat, bright sky was very strange.

He often called the country the evening land in his mind, because of the eternal twilight, but he now thought that name was wrong. Evening is the time of change, the threshold of night.

The soft wind blowing down the valley of the creek roughened the surface of the pool. The vision touched him again: the broad dim step, the threshold land, and this silver stream across it running downward into darkness from what heights, what eastern mountains of unimaginable day?

He sat again bewildered in the twilight, feeling that he

had known for a moment why he held that water to be sacred.

"I ought to go on," he said under his breath. Every now and then he spoke, half aloud, alone; a word or a sentence once in a whole stay.

He had been shaving, and he got on with it. What seemed a day and a night's worth here might be less than an hour in the daylight world, but his beard kept his time, not the clock's. It would have simplified life to let the thing grow—though at eighteen he had worried about it, it was thick, vigorous, and brassy now, so that his mother was always telling him he needed to shave—but employees of Sam's Thrift-E-Mart were not permitted to wear beards. He had had enough hassle about keeping his hair where he liked it, down about to his collar. So the last of his ritual at the willow place, before he packed up and hid his gear, was the shave. Sometimes he heated water, but if his fire had gone out he used cold water, clenched his teeth and scraped away; even then the touch of that water was kindly.

On Saturday night he told his mother he would be gone all Sunday morning on a long hike "in the country." She complained again about the noise he made getting up early, but was not otherwise interested. He left at five in the morning, with a packet under his arm of expensive dried and freeze-dried food to transfer to his pack. He intended to stay a while in the twilight land, to leave what he knew, to go on.

He had never found but one path that seemed to be a real path or way: the one that led out of the beginning place, directly away from the gateway. He crossed from rock to rock at the ford, went past the dark bushes that the girl had stepped out of, a long time ago now, weeks, and started up the slope out of the valley of the creek. The path climbed, winding a bit but keeping on the axis vertical to the creek, the one direction he hoped to be able to keep. He had found that, even when momentarily disoriented in the woods upstream, if he stopped and let it come to him he had a general sense of where the gateway was—behind him, to the left, over that rise, or whatever—and this sense had not yet played him false. He had no plan now but to keep the gateway directly behind him if he could, and to go on until he was tired of going.

Up on the crest of the ridge the air seemed lighter. On the far slope the trees were tall and sparse, the ground between them open, without underbrush. Faint but clear enough to the searching eye, the path ran straight on down. As he followed it over the ridgetop he lost for the first time the sound of the creek, the voice that blessed his sleep.

He walked for a long way, steadily and rather doggedly, taking some pride and pleasure in his body's ready endurance. The path grew no clearer but no less clear. Other ways branched off from it, deer trails most likely, but there was never any doubt which was the main one. He knew that if he turned around this path would take him straight back to the beginning place. His sense of where the gateway was seemed almost to sharpen as he went farther from it, as if its psychic law of gravity were the opposite of the physical one.

After crossing a creek somewhat smaller than the gateway creek he sat down near the noisy water and had a bit to eat; when he went on he felt cheerful, resolved to trust his luck.

All the folds of the land ran across his way. The valleys were dim; in the depth of the dimness always there was the voice of a spring or stream. The slopes were not difficult climbing but they got larger and higher as he went on, the upslopes always longer than the downslopes, as if all the land was tilted. When he came to a third big creek he stopped to have a swim, and after swimming decided to call it a day. He liked the phrase. It was perfectly accurate. He could take any piece of time he liked and call it a day; another span and call it night, and sleep it through. He

65

had never (he thought, sitting by the coals of his brushwood fire on the shore of the creek) experienced time before. He had let clocks do it for him. Clocks were what kept things going, there on the other side; business hours, traffic lights, plane schedules, lovers' meetings, summit meetings, world wars, there was no carrying on without clocks; all the same, clock time had about the same relation to unclock time as a two-by-four or a box of toothpicks has to a fir tree. Here there was no use asking, "What time is it?" because there was nothing to answer for you, no sun saying "Noon" and no clock saying "Seven-thirty-eight and forty-two seconds." You had to answer the question yourself and the answer was "Now."

He slept, and dreamed of nothing, and woke slowly, so relaxed he could hardly raise his hand at first.

From this third creek on, the land got rougher. The tilt of it was all up, and the tiny streams now chased downward beside or across the trail. The trail itself was clear. Whoever had made it, whenever it had been made, there was no litter, no sign of any recent passer, but the way was unmistakable, going up easily and purposefully, turning back and forth on the slopes but always heading the same general direction. Its purpose was all he had; he let it lead him. The forest had thickened, massive stands of fir, where the twilight lay heavy. There was no sound but the soughing of wind in the firs, an immense quiet noise. He crossed the small trails of rabbits or mice or other shy wood creatures, once he saw a tiny broken skull near the path, but he saw no living creature. It was as if each here kept its own solitude. The sense of his solitude came on him now as he climbed the long, dim slopes in the unchanging quiet. He saw himself, very small, walking through the wilderness from no place to no place, alone. So he might walk on forever. For the time beyond the clocks is always now and the way to forever is now.

Hunger broke his trance of walking. He stopped to eat;

when he went on he felt less dreamy, more alert. The trail now got so steep in places that he leaned forward on both hands to rest, and he felt the mountain press against his hands, the bulk and depth and strength of the earth, her grainy skin rough with rocks and roots. For a long time the trail had been going somewhat left of the gateway axis. Now it turned back towards the axis and leveled out. He could stand straight and walk freely, and the easier rhythm was a relief. The firs crowded thick, high, and dark, the air under them was dark, but as he looked ahead he saw the clear breadth of the trail, almost a road here. And in the dry air he caught, once, once again, the faint scent of woodsmoke.

Now he walked steadily, alert, intent.

The road swung in a long rising curve, on and on. The slopes to the right below it steepened and began to drop away so sharply that the trees below the road no longer blocked the view. He could for the first time in this land see for a long way. He saw that he was on the side of a mountain. To his right and ahead, beyond a falling sweep of treetops, the rim of a farther mountain stood dark against the clarity of sky. He walked on more slowly, a little dazed, feeling himself as if floating between the vast, obscure valleys and the vast gulfs of the sky. He looked along the road as it turned again, and saw nestled against the mountain shoulder the roofs and chimneys of a town, the gleam of a lighted window in the cold dusk. There was home, and he walked towards it, and came down the street between the lamp-lit windows, hearing a child's voice calling words he did not understand.

4

In daylight he did not look so big, and he was younger than she had thought, her own age or younger, a heavy, stoop-shouldered, white-faced boy. He was stupid, not understanding anything she said. "I need to come back," he said, as if asking her permission, as if she could or would permit him. "I'm trying to warn you," she said, but he did not understand, and she could bear it no longer. She had walked from Mountain Town to the gateway and was tired from that and from the anger and terror of this confrontation with him, and she had to go on and get home, clean up, eat, get to work—Patsi would be asking where she'd spent the night—it was broad daylight, Wednesday, she had promised to take her mother's stuff to the dry cleaner's. He stood there, the charcoal of her sign smeared on his face, the contemptible enemy, and she had to leave him there and go, not knowing if she would find the way open to her when she came back.

It was earlier than she had thought. She got to the apartment a little after six. Rick and Patsi had not been talking to each other for a couple of days, and she got included in their vindictive silence, so no questions were asked about where she had spent the night. When she got back from work that evening, Patsi continued to interpret her night's absence as a sign of disloyalty, and loftily ignored it; Rick alluded to it only for his own purposes—"Shit, what does anybody want to sleep *here* for?"

She had been glad to move in with Rick and Patsi last fall. They were generous without overdoing the sharing bit, and liked the place clean enough to live in but not clean enough to drive you up the wall. Her paying a third of the rent was important to them since Rick wasn't working. It had been a good arrangement, and still would be, except that Rick and Patsi were breaking up, and so no arrangement that involved them as a couple could be good. The worst of it now was that Rick wanted to use her against Patsi, and her staying out a night and offering no explanation gave him the idea that she might be available for more than a phony pass. All she had to say was that she'd spent the night at her mother's place, but she didn't want to stoop to lying to him; he no longer deserved the honor of a lie. He kept trying to come into her room and talk. On Thursday night he kept at it, it was serious, he said, they had to discuss the future, Patsi wasn't willing to talk seriously but somebody had to. Not me, Irene thought. Rick, a thin fellow of twenty-five covered with reddish, curly hair like a well-worn Teddy bear, stood with lounging persistence between her and the door to her room. He wore only a pair of jeans with the worn-through knees gaping open weirdly. His toes were very long and thin. "I don't feel like talking about anything specially," Irene said, but he went on, talking through his nose about how somebody around here had to talk sometime and he wanted to explain some things about him and Patsi that Irene ought to know.

"Not tonight," Irene said, slamming a kitchen drawer, and bolted past him into her room and shut the door. He lounged around the kitchen for a while swearing and then slammed his way out of the apartment. Patsi, in the other bedroom, slammed nothing, maintaining a righteous silence.

Irene sat on the edge of her bed with her shoulders hunched forward and her hands between her knees and thought, This can't last. End of the month, we've had it. Then where?

She had been lucky, being able to stay out here near her mother and paying only one-third rent. She had been able to pay off the car, which her job for Mott and Zerming depended on, and pay for a brake job and two new tires. She could afford to pay more for rent, but not as much as an efficiency out here would cost. The thing to do would be move into the city, downtown, and pay about half as much, but then her mother would worry about her getting raped and hassled; and it would take half an hour or forty minutes to get out here, so she would worry about her mother. If only she would call when Victor got drunk. But she wouldn't call.

Irene got up and went out, slamming the front door a little, and walked over to see her mother.

It was a hot, still night. A lot of people were out. Chelsea Gardens Avenue was a roar of cars gunning, idling, drag racing, cruising. At the farm, Victor had rigged up a flood-light so he could work on his car in the front yard. There was no reason why he should do it at night, he had the whole day and was no good at fixing cars anyhow, Irene had taken auto shop and knew twice as much as he did about engines; but he liked to be in the spotlight. He had a wrench in one hand and a beer can in the other and was yelling at the boys, "Get the fuck away from those tools, you little bastards!" Two or three of his sons, Irene's half brothers, rushed past her through the glare and darkness of the yard. They paid no attention to her arrival, but the dogs did, the three little dogs yapping hysterically at her ankles and the crazy Doberman that Victor kept chained up choking off his terrible bark by lunging on his chain. Irene's mother was in the cavernous kitchen with Treese, the four-year-old. Treese was at the table eating chocolate-flavored cereal from the package while her mother moved slowly about collecting the dinner dishes to wash. It was nine o'clock. "Hello, Irena my darling," Mrs. Hanson said with a slow, happy smile, and they hugged each other.

Mary Hanson was thirty-nine years old and had had three miscarriages and six pregnancies carried to term. Michael and Irene were the children of her first husband, Nick Pannis, dead of leukemia three months after Michael's birth. Nick's aunt had taken in the young widow and her babies. The aunt owned the farmhouse and a share in the tree nursery across the road, where she worked. When she retired and took her savings to a mobile home in Florida, she gave the farmhouse and its half acre to Mary. Shortly after that Victor Hanson moved in, married Mary, and begot Wayne, then Dalton, then David, then Treese and the miscarriages. Victor had theories about many things, including sex, and liked to expound them to people: "See, if the man doesn't get rid of the fertile material, you understand what I mean, the fertile cells, they back up and cause the prostrate gland. That material has to be cleared out regularly or they make poison, same as anything doesn't get cleared out regularly. Same as clean bowels, or blowing your nose, if you don't blow your nose you can get impacted sinus trouble." Victor was a big, well-made, handsome man, much concerned with his body and its functions and appearance, a central reality of which the rest of the world and other people were mere reflections without substance: the self-concern of the athlete or the invalid, though he was neither, being healthy and inactive. He had worked for an aluminum-siding company, but the job disappeared after a while. Sometimes he worked for a friend who sold used cars. Sometimes he went off with friends named Don and Fred, or Dwight and Roy, who were in the TV repair business or the auto-parts business; he would come back with some money, always in cash. From time to time a lot of bicycles were stored in the old tractor shed, which he kept padlocked. The little boys were crazy to get at the bikes, good

71

ten-speeds, new-looking, but he knocked Dalton across the room once for even mentioning the bicycles, which he was storing as a favor for his friend Dwight.

Michael, at fourteen, discovered that his stepfather had gone in for drug pushing in a small way, and was keeping his supplies, mostly speed, in Mary's chest of drawers. He and Irene discussed turning him in to the police. They finally flushed the stuff down the toilet and said nothing to anybody. How could they talk to the cops when they couldn't even talk to their mother? There was no telling what she knew and did not know; the word "know," in this situation, grew hard to define. The one certain fact was, she was loyal. Victor was her husband. What he did was all right with her.

Michael was her first-born son, and what he did was all right too. But he would not accept that. It was immoral. If she had stayed loyal to his dead father, then her loyalty to him would have counted; but she had remarried. . . . At seventeen Michael moved out, having got a job with a construction firm on the other side of the city. Irene had seen him only twice in the two years since.

As children she and Michael, less than two years apart in age, had been very close in spirit, sharing their world entirely. When he got to be about eleven Michael began to turn away from her, which seemed right or inevitable to her and so was a loss but no heavy grief; but as he came into full adolescence his rejection of her had become absolute. He spent his time with a male clique, adopting all their manner and rhetoric of contempt for the female, and sparing her none of it. This, which she could only feel as betrayal, happened at about the same time that her stepfather began to get really pushy, waylaying her on the way to the bathroom upstairs, pressing himself against her when he passed her in the kitchen, coming into her bedroom without knocking, trying to get his hand up her skirt. Once he caught her behind the tractor shed, and she tried to joke with him and make fun of him, because she could not believe he was serious until he was all over her suddenly heavy as a mattress, smothering and brutal, and she got away with a moment of luck and a sprained wrist. After that she knew never to be alone in the house with him and not to go into the back yard at all. It was hard always to be worrying about that. She wanted to tell Michael and get some support from him, a little help. But she couldn't tell him now. He would despise her for allowing, inviting, Victor to hassle her. He already despised her for it, for being a woman, therefore subject to lust, therefore unclean.

So long as Michael lived at home, if she had actually yelled for help he would have come to her help. But if she yelled then her mother would know, and she didn't want her mother to know. Mary's life was built upon, consisted of, her love and loyalty, her family. To break those bonds would be to break her. If she had to choose, forced to it, she would probably stand up for her daughter against her husband: and then Victor would have all the excuse to punish her he wanted. Once Michael left, the only thing Irene could do was leave too. But she could not just clear out, like Michael, so long, been good to know you. Her mother had to have somebody around to depend on. She had had four pregnancies in the last five years, three of them ending in miscarriage. She was on the pill now but Victor didn't know it because he believed that contraception "blocked the fertile material up in the glands" and forbade her to use contraceptives, which she probably wouldn't do if Irene wasn't there to encourage her and make a woman's mystery of it. She had circulatory troubles; she had pyorrhea and needed major dental work, which she could get cheap at the Dental School, but only if somebody was willing to drive her clear out there every Saturday. Victor hit her around when he was drunk, not dangerously so far, though once he had dislocated her shoulder. Nobody was there with her most of the time but the children, and if she got seriously hurt or ill nobody might do anything about it at all.

She said to her daughter, with the tenderness that had to replace honesty between them, "Honey, why do you stick around out in this old dump? You ought to get a room downtown where you work, and be with some nice young people. It used to be nice out here, but these suburbs, housing developments, trash."

Irene would defend her arrangement with Patsi and Rick.

"Patsi Sobotny, is that what you call a friend!"

Mary disapproved absolutely of Patsi for living with Rick unmarried. Once, exasperated, Irene had shouted at her, "What's so great about marriage, according to you?" Mary had taken the attack straight on, without defense. She had stood still a minute, gazing across the dark kitchen at the window, and answered, "I don't know, Irena. I'm old-fashioned, I think like people used to think, I know. But your father, see. Nick. It was—with him, you know, the sex, that was beautiful, you know, I can't say it, but it was just one part. There was the whole thing. Everything else, your whole life, the world, see, is a part of it, like it's a part of you, being a husband and wife like that. I don't know how to say it. Once you know what it's like, like that, once you felt that, nothing else makes so very much difference."

Irene was silent, seeing in her mother's face some hint of that central glory; seeing also the fearful fact that all the glory can happen and be done with by the age of twenty-two, and one can live for twenty, thirty, fifty years after that, work and marry and bear children and all the rest, without any particular reason to do so, without desire.

I am the daughter of a ghost, Irene thought.

Tonight, as she helped her mother clean up the kitchen, she told her that Patsi and Rick were on the way to breaking up. "So kick out that no-good Rick and you and Patsi find some nice girl to share with," Mary suggested, enlisting promptly on the women's side.

"I don't think Patsi'll want to. I don't much want to go on rooming with her either."

"Better than nobody," Mary said. "You go around too much by yourself, you never have any fun, my baby. Hiking in the country by yourself! You ought to be dancing, not hiking. Or anyhow get into some kind of hiking club where there's nice young people."

"You got nice young people on the brain, mama."

"Somebody has to have brains," Mary said with calm self-satisfaction. She came up behind Irene at the sink and stroked her hair softly, making it into a cloudy, twisted mane. "Terrible hair you got. Greek hair, just like mine. You ought to move downtown. This is a dump out here."

"You live here."

"For me it's right. For you not."

The three boys irrupted into the kitchen and at once made Treese cry by grabbing her box of cereal and stuffing their mouths. They were so cataclysmic as a group that it was always surprising to find that, one at a time, each was a mousy little boy with a husky, mumbling voice. Mary had no control over anything they did outside the house, and they ran wild; indoors her sense of decorum prevailed over all the mindless disorder of their existence, and they obeyed her. She cleared them straight off to watch television, and turned back to her elder daughter. She was smiling, the slow, happy smile that showed her bad teeth and gums. She told the good news, the news too good to tell at once, too good to put off telling any longer: "Michael telephoned."

"What did he say?"

"Just how he was, and he asked about everybody here, you and everybody. He's got a car, too."

"Why doesn't he drive it over to see us?"

"He's working very hard," said the mother, turning away to close the doors of the dish cupboard.

So he's working hard, Irene thought, he could come see his mother once a year. But telephoning's a big enough favor for Big Mister Man to do. And Mister Man's mother laps it up and says thanks. . . .

I can't take it, I really can't take it any more. Now I just hurt mama saying that about why doesn't he drive over to see us. Everybody I know just hurts each other. All the time. I have got to get out. I can't keep coming home. Next time Victor tries to cop a feel or even touches me or treats her like shit I'm going to blow, I can't shut up any more, and that'll just make it worse and hurt her more, and I can't do anything, and I can't take it. Love! What good is love? I love her. I love Michael, just like she does. So what? God help me, I'll never fall in love, never be in love, never love anybody. Love is just a fancy word for how to hurt somebody worse. I want to get out. Clear out, clear out, clear out.

That night when she left her mother she did not go down the road to Chelsea Gardens, but turned left from the house, walking up the gravel road till she was out of the glare of Victor's floodlight and then cutting off left again across the fields. It was unpleasant walking in the dark, for the ground was hard and uneven under the tangled grass, and she carried no flashlight for fear of attracting the attention of a bunch of leatherjackets or the suburban weirdo gang that sometimes hung around near the factory. The same stupid fear that spoiled all walks alone since her school friend Doris had been raped by a gang in a half-built house in Chelsea Gardens, the stupid fear that left no free place except the sweet desolation of the ain country.

But in the woods the path did not lead down between the laurels and the pine into the clear, eternal evening. It was warm, dark; crickets sang loud and soft, near and far; under that singing was a heavy, continual sound or vibration, cars on the highway perhaps or the sound of the whole city, whose glow in the heavy night sky made it possible to walk even here in the woods. But there was no sound of water running. She walked a few steps past where the threshold should have been, and then turned back. There was no way.

She remembered then how she had watched him go through the gate, across the threshold, the heavy stranger, how he had walked on and the twilight had flowed on before him like a wave. That had been frightening; she did not like to think of it. It had been his fault. It had happened to him, not to her. She could always get back. She had brought him back. It was from this side that she could not always cross.

Could he? Was he there now, where she could not come?

Dogged, she came back to Pincus's woods the next afternoon after work, and every two or three days for a week, two weeks, as if it were a contest that must be won by willpower, by refusal to give up. At the end of the second week she began to drive every afternoon after work first to the paint factory parking lot, leave the car there, and cross the fields to the wood. She found she was beating a path in the dry August grass and changed her route, going round about one way or another each time, so as to leave no track for others, that other, to follow. But there was nothing to hide. The woods; blackberry thickets; a path; a culvert; after a while a barbed-wire fence straggling across the foot of a hill among the trees. A couple of sparrows chirping, the faint drum of the cars on the highway, and the sound of the city like the breathing of an animal thirty miles long, so big you couldn't hear it. The hot, late sunshine and the soft, bluish air. Usually she stood a minute where the path came down, where the threshold should have been, then turned around, plodded back across the fields to her car, drove to the apartment, a few blocks west of Chelsea Gardens Avenue.

Patsi and Rick had been having a hectic sexual reconciliation, the last flare-up. On a Saturday night after a visit with her mother she got back in the middle of the biggest fight yet. She could not get out of it. She was part of the family. When Patsi accused Rick of sleeping with Irene she had to defend him and herself; when Rick accused Patsi of not sharing fair on the money she had to stand up for Patsi, who then turned on her for pushing everybody around. After hours and hours of it she realised that the only thing to do, and she should have done it hours ago, was to pack up, pay up, and get out.

Patsi and Rick were sullen, shellshocked. Patsi made an elaborately fair division of the raspberry preserves they had put up together last month, insisting that Irene take exactly half the jars; she kept crying, tears rolling slowly down her cheeks, but she did not say goodbye. Rick helped Irene carry her stuff down to the car and kept saying, "Ah, shit. Well, shit." It was after eight on Sunday morning when Irene got away. She drove her car, loaded with her worldly goods in two grocery cartons and a handleless suitcase, down Chelsea Gardens Avenue and Chelsea Gardens Place across the road to the farm. The three little dogs began to yap and the Doberman to bellow at the sound of the car in the Sunday-morning silence. Except for the dogs, the farmhouse, surrounded by gutted automobile carcasses, looked derelict. She backed out of the yard, turned right on the gravel road, drove to the parking lot below the paint factory, and parked there. She locked the car and set off once more across the weedy fields already simmering in the heat of what was going to be a fierce day. If the way's closed I'll wait there, she thought. I'll sit down and wait there till it opens. I don't care if it takes a month. . . .

She was crazy-headed from the endless night of quarreling, arguing, explaining, recriminating, excusing. She had had no breakfast, though between four and five A.M. she had eaten a box of pretzel sticks and drunk a quart of milk while Rick was telling Patsi how she played power games and she was telling him that he was a male chauvinist. . . . I'll go to sleep there in front of the threshold, and wake up every now and then and see if it's open yet, Irene told herself. Open, open, open, the word jolted in her head as her steps jolted her body. Hot daylight glared in her eyes. Open, eyes. Open, door. There's the woods, there's the way into the woods. There's the ditch, there's the ivy patch. There's the big thicket, there's the path down, the pine with the red trunk, the gateway and the gate, the opened door, the way into my country, my own country, my heart's home.

She entered into the twilight. She drank from the stream, then crossed and went a little way upriver to a nook sheltered by two big elder bushes where, years ago, she had used to sleep. She lay down there, and made a little moaning sob in pure weariness and the bewilderment of a wish fulfilled; and slept.

Sleep in the ain country was so deep it had no dreams. I am the dream, she thought drowsily, the dream am I. I am the mare but there's no night. What's that?—and she was awake sitting bolt upright and her heart pounding, for it had been a noise that waked her, a high gobbling scream far off in the woods—had there been a noise?

Nothing but the sound of water running and the sighing of wind high up in the trees. The sky was quiet. Nothing moved in the forest.

After a while she stood up cautiously, looking about her

for any sign of change, of danger. It's his fault, she thought, that fat face, that slug. He's changed everything. It's not the same any more. She was glad to give her uneasiness a cause, and a detestable cause. But as she looked about for traces of the intruder, his hearthplace, his pack, and saw nothing, she was in no way relieved of fear. Her heart went on pounding, her breath came short. What am I afraid of? she demanded, outraged. Here, here of all places? It's the same as ever, the safe place. I must have had a dream, a bad dream. I want to go to Tembreabrezi. I wish I was there now, indoors, in the inn. I'm hungry. That's what's wrong with me, I'm hungry.

She drank again long and deep to fill her stomach, and picked stalks of mint to chew as she went, and set off on the way to Mountain Town. She went lightfoot as always, lighter and faster than ever, for hunger drove her, and fear drove her, and she could not afford to stop and think about either one, for if she did they became unbearable. So long as she kept going she need not think, and the dusk forest flowed past her like the water of the streams; so light, so fast she went that nothing would hear her steps, nothing would notice her, nothing would rise up before her on the path closing the way to her with white, wrinkled arms.

There were candles in the windows of the inn, as if they were expecting her. No one was in the street. It must be late, suppertime or past. At the thought of supper, of soup, bread, stew, porridge, anything, anything at all to eat, she felt her head spin; and when Sofir opened the inn door to her and there was warmth and light and the smell of cooking and the sound of his deep voice, she found it difficult to keep standing up. "Oh, Sofir," she said, "I am so hungry!"

At the sound of her voice Palizot came, and though she was a woman not lavish of gesture, she kissed Irene and held her for a moment.

"We have been afraid for you," Sofir said. He steered

her in to sit by the fire. It was late indeed: the company of the inn had all gone home, the fire had sunk down. Sofir and Palizot bustled about getting water for her to wash in, food for her to eat, talking away. "And you know he's come!" Palizot said, and Irene said, "Who has come?"

The two well-known, well-loved faces turned to her in the jubilant firelight; Palizot looked to Sofir smiling, giving him the word for them both. "It's him," Sofir said, "he's here now. Things will go better now!"—with such warmth of pleasure and such certainty of Irene's sharing in that pleasure that she was unable to say anything. "There now, it's hot," said Palizot, serving up a plate for her, at sight of which Irene ceased to care about anything else whatever. Lapped in present bliss, food, rest, firelight, friendship, she ate; and then Sofir had her room ready for her, the room that looked out over the dark drop and reach of the forests to the eastern ridge.

Sofir was out and Palizot occupied, so she breakfasted alone. There was not much to breakfast on: a little thin milk, a pot of cheese, and a loaf so hard and small, compared to the round brown splendors of Sofir's baking in other days, that she hardly had the heart to cut a slice off the poor wizened thing. Clearly, no wheat had come up the mountain from the merchants of the King's City.

She had thought as she woke that when Sofir and Palizot said "he," last night, "he has come," they meant the King. A little wider awake, she had thought they had not meant the King himself, but a messenger from the King, somebody sent with the power to open the roads. Awake, she knew they had meant nothing of the kind.

"You'll be going up to the Master's house," said Palizot, coming through the kitchen with an armload of clothing from the wash lines. "I freshened up your red dress a bit; it gets so creased lying in the chest. Have you got clean stockings? Look, how do you like these?"

"I suppose he's there," Irene said. Since "he" was not

staying at the inn, he must have been invited, as she had never been, to stay at the Master's house. Her pain, a sore one however petty its cause, and her determination not to show it, so preoccupied her that for a minute she did not absorb Palizot's reply: "He? Oh, no, he's at the manor. But the Master asked us a long time ago to tell you to come to him as soon as you could, whenever you came again."

That was balm. "He" could stay at the manor all he pleased.

"They're beautiful," she said, admiring the fine-striped stockings Palizot was exhibiting atop the load of clothes. "You just knitted them?"

"From the good wool in four old pairs I unraveled," Palizot said with the satisfaction of the canny artisan. "Wear them today, levadja. They're for you."

In the handsome stockings and the red dress Irene went out into the twilight of the street, and climbed the hiccuping steps to the Master's house. The geese in the pen by the south wall, big creatures, their white necks and bodies vague and as if luminous, shifted and hissed; one beat its wings for an instant. She had always been a little afraid of the geese. She knocked at the twelve-paneled door and Fimol, calm as always, admitted her and took her across the hall, between the mournful stare of the ancestress and the scowl of the one-armed ancestor, to the door of the Master's office. "Irena has come," Fimol said in her clear, subdued voice. He turned from his desk, holding out his hands with open gladness: "Irena, Irenadja! Welcome! We have longed for you!"

I have longed for you, she wanted to say, but could not. Her tongue never would obey her, in the Master's presence. It obeyed him.

"Come and sit down," he said. His smile made him look young. His voice was kind. "Tell me, how was it for you coming here? Was the way clear? Was it hard for you?" His dark gaze was directly on her now. "I've been afraid you would not be able to come," he said, speaking lower and hurriedly, and looked away.

"The gate was closed—until last night. I wanted—I tried to come!"

He nodded, grave and gentle.

She tried to get the right words. "I saw nothing, when the way opened—nothing was different. But I felt— There was a noise, maybe I didn't hear it. There was something that I know I didn't see—"

As she spoke, now, in this quiet room, the terror she had not allowed herself to feel yesterday coming through the forests on the mountainside came running through her body in one long, cold shockwave: she crouched and shuddered in her chair. Her voice went thin and dry. "I was never afraid in the forest before!"

She looked up into the Master's dark face, wanting the reassurance of his strength. He said nothing for a while; then at last, his voice still muted. "Yet you came."

"Someone else—Sofir said—someone else has come, a man—"

The Master nodded. He was concealing or constrained by some intensity of emotion. Finally he said a word or name Irene did not know, *hiuradja,* and met her gaze again, intense, questioning.

"Did he come from the north—from the City?" she asked, though she knew the answer.

"From the south. Like you. On the south road. As you first came, not knowing the land or language."

Curiosity, the wish to know the full flatness of the truth, was stronger than disappointment or resentment. "Is he—" She did not know the word for blond or fair; they were a dark people. "Has he straw hair, and he's fat?"

The Master gave his brief nod.

"We are summoned to the manor to meet him," he said, and something in his voice alerted Irene, a hint of irony, of anger—resentment? "Come."

"Now?"

83

"As soon as may be, Lord Horn said." Again that hint of dryness, or sarcasm; but he exchanged no glance of complicity with her, and impenetrable as ever led her out of his house and across the top of the street to the high, delicate, open gates that led to the manor. He did not speak as they walked between the lawns and groves. To their right the slopes of the mountain rose up, darkly forested, yielding one glimpse of the slanting rock faces of the distant summit. Before them stood the great house, built of a tawny stone in which a warmth lingered like the light of sunset, the afterglow.

An old man let them in and took them through cold, half-furnished, stately rooms, and upstairs to a many-windowed gallery. The windows looked east, over the great downward slope to the distant eastern ridges distinct against the sky. A fire burned in a marble fireplace at the far end of the gallery, and there Lord Horn and his daughter stood with the stranger.

It was him, of course, the dough face, the heavy hands. She glanced at the man beside her: the dark, hard, fine profile, controlled, contained, vigorous. The Master said nothing, made no least gesture, but she knew his hatred as clearly as she knew her own.

Lord Horn had come forward in his stiff, slow way to greet them. The daughter was smiling pallidly. She was blonde, Irene had forgotten that; they were not all dark-haired after all. This girl's hair was pale and fleecy like sheep's wool.

"Irena, our friend," Lord Horn said. "Our guest, your countryman, I think. He is called Hiuradjas."

She saw him recognise her—the light dawning: dismay, then surprise, then hope, like a doubletake in a TV comedy. He stepped forward with heavy eagerness and said, in English, stammering, "Hi, I—I'm sorry it—I don't know their language, like you said."

She stepped back a pace, keeping her distance.

84

"Lord Horn," she said, "when I am here I speak the language spoken here." The intruder and the mealy-madonna-faced girl stared, and the Master grew alert as a hawk, as she knew from the turn of his head; but Horn said nothing; only he looked, slowly as always, at the Master. There was a curious silence, difficult to bear.

"He cannot speak our language," the old man said. "Will you help us speak together?"

The Master made no sign. The old lord's gravity was impressive. Unwilling and ungracious she turned to face the intruder, not looking at him but at the polished floor in front of his shoes—tennis shoes, large, long, and dirty. "They want me to translate for you. Go on."

"I know you don't like my being here," the young man's voice said. "I don't belong here, I guess. I don't know. My name's Hugh Rogers. If you tell them anything I'm saying, tell them thank you. They've been very kind to me."

When his voice stuck she could hear it creak in his throat.

"He says he came here by mistake," she said, turning towards Lord Horn, but not looking up as she spoke. "He wishes to thank you for your kindness." She kept her voice neutral, a translating machine.

"He is welcome to us, thrice welcome."

"He says you're welcome," she said in English, expressionless.

"Who is he? I don't even know their names. You're Rayna?"

That threw her off stride for a moment. He would call her Eye-reen. No one but her mother and the people of Mountain Town called her Irena. But he had heard her name from them, of course. It was none of his business anyway. "That is Aur Horn—Lord Horn. That is Dou Sark, Master Sark, the Master of Tembreabrezi. That is Horn's daughter. I don't know her name."

"Allia," the girl said unexpectedly, with a simper, speaking not to Irene but to Hugh Rogers. He turned his sheepish look on her, then back to Irene.

"I think they think I'm somebody I'm not," he said.

She did not help him out.

"Can you tell them that I don't belong here—that I come from, you know, somewhere else, and it's a mistake."

"I can say that. It won't change anything."

Her contempt had finally stung him. He straightened up from his slouch, frowning. "Look," he said, "when I got here, it was like they were waiting for me. They act like they know who I am. But I don't know them and I can't make them understand that they've got me mixed up with somebody else that I'm not."

"You don't know who you are, here."

"They don't. I do," he said with unexpected solidity.

"It's the way you came."

"I didn't *come,* I just got here, I didn't know there was a town, I just followed a path!"

"None of them can walk on that path. Nobody here. Only people that come from—through the gate."

He did not take this in. "Can't you just tell them that whoever it is they're expecting, I'm not him?"

She turned to Lord Horn and said, "He bids me tell you that he is not that man you wait for."

"We take him for no other man than himself," the old man said quietly. There were double or shadow meanings in the words he used. She turned them into English hesitantly: "Lord Horn says you are who you say you are, as far as they're concerned."

"I seem to be who *they* say I am."

"What's wrong with that?" she sneered.

"I have to go back soon. Do they know that?"

"They won't stop you."

"You warned me—back at the gate—that time. What of? Are they dangerous? Are they in danger?"

"Yes."

86

"Which? What kind of danger?"

"Both. Why should I tell you? Do I owe you something? You said yourself you don't belong here. You're the danger, you're what's wrong, it began when you came. I do belong here, this is my place. You think I'm going to hand it over to you because you're a man and own everything. Well, it's not that way here!"

"Irena," the Master said, beside her, "What is it? What has he said?"

"Nothing! He's a fool. He doesn't belong here, he shouldn't be here. You must send him away and forbid him to come back!"

"What is this?" Lord Horn said, slowly as ever. "Do you not know this man, Irena?"

"No. I don't know him, I will not know him!"

Allia spoke to her father in her light, even voice: "Irena speaks in fear for us."

Lord Horn looked at his daughter, at Sark, at Irene. His eyes, the almost colorless eyes of an old man, held hers.

"We call you friend," he said.

"I am your friend," she said fiercely.

"You are. And he. No harm comes by that road, your road, Irena. You came to speak our word, he to serve our need; this is as it is to be. One and other, other and one. It is two that go that road."

She stood silent, frightened.

"I go alone," she whispered.

Then the stupid tears rose up in her eyes and she had to turn her back until she could control herself and had wiped her nose and eyes with the handkerchief Palizot had put in the pocket of her dress. It was hard to turn around and face them. Her face burned as she did so.

"I will try to do what you ask me to do," she said. "What do you want me to say to him?"

"What seems best to you," Lord Horn replied in his muted, steady tone. "You speak for us."

To her bewilderment he stood back for Allia and grim-faced Sark, and with the slightest stiff nod to her and to Hugh Rogers followed them out of the room. She was left face to face with the stranger.

He sat down on a chair that was too narrow for him, then got up awkwardly and went to stand at the high windows.

"I'm sorry," he said.

The eastern light was cold. She moved closer to the hearth. The spasm of tears had left her cold and dull. She must do what she had promised to do.

"This is what they want to say to you, as far as I understand it. There's something wrong here, there's some reason they can't leave the town. Nobody can walk on the roads. Except us coming from the south. They're afraid of something and it seems to keep getting worse. Until you came; they think that's going to change it some way."

"Change what?"

"This fear."

"What fear? This is where I'm not afraid." He turned from the window. "I don't understand anything here, the language, why it's never night or sunlight, but it's never frightened me. What is there to be afraid of?"

"I don't know. I don't speak the language all that well. They won't talk about it or I don't understand when they do. They just say they can't leave the town and nobody can come here from the plains."

"The plains," he repeated.

"Northward, down the mountain. The road goes across the plains to a city finally."

She looked at him and saw his eyes, grey-blue or blue, wide, in the heavy, white, yearning face. He had turned to her but he did not see her, he was looking in his mind across the plains of the twilight.

"Have you gone there?"

She shook her head.

"Which way is the sea?"

"I don't know. I don't know the word for sea."

"The creeks all run west," he said in a low voice. He looked at her with the anxious, bewildered look he had, like a steer, the wrinkled forehead and curly hair, blunt face, worried eye. There had been a picture on the cover of a book once long ago, a man with a bull's head standing in a tiny room. It had come back to her in the darkness before sleep many times, the man's body and the terrible heavy head.

"Do you know where we are?" he said, and she said, "No."

After a while he said, "I have to go soon. I'm worried about being late getting back. Next weekend I can come overnight, it's the long weekend. If they want me to do something. I can try.—Overnight clock time, I mean. Do you—do you figure it's about an hour clock time to something like a day here, I mean a day and a night, if it . . ."

"If there was any day or night," she confirmed. It was very strange to speak of anything like this with another person, to hear him speak of it. "How did you get through the gate, the first time?" she asked in pure curiosity, and asking knew she had wasted all her rage, had accepted the fact that he was here and let him know it.

"I was . . ." He blinked. His voice made the little creaking sound in his throat. "I was running away. From . . . I don't know. See, I'm sort of stuck. Not doing what I want to do."

"What do you want to do?"

"Nothing. Important." It came out in two separate words. "It's just I want to go to school, but I can't work it in."

"What kind of school?"

"Library. It isn't that important."

"Well, if it's what you want to do with your life it is. What do you do?"

"Checker at a grocery."

89

"Yeah."

"It's good pay. It's O.K. You know. How did you get here first?"

"Running away. Too."

But her throat dried up. She couldn't talk about all that, Doris getting raped, and all the hassle at home, and all that, it was a long time ago now and there wasn't any use talking about it. She had got away from it. She had come here. None of that existed here. Here was peace, and silence, and nothing changed, it was always the same. Here you did not ask questions. You came home. He could not understand that, he was a stranger. She could not tell him that she came here because her love was here. Her love, her master. No one would ever know that, no one would ever understand it, that center and secret of her life, that silence. In his age, in his mastery, in his strangeness, in his hardness even, in all that divided them, in the distance that held them apart, there was room for desire without terror, there was room and time for love without effect, without penalty or pain. The only price was silence.

She was silent.

The stranger, massive against the window light, stood half turned from her, looking out.

"I wish I could stay," he said half aloud.

But he turned away from the window, resolute; and went to take his leave of his hosts. She stayed only to give his assurance that he would come back to Lord Horn, who accepted both his parting and his promise to return without question, and then she left the manor. As she walked between the lawns to the iron gate she thought of the return trip she too must soon make. She looked at the dark mountain flank, the remote grey of the rock faces. The silence of the mountain was heavy, like a lid pressed down on a sound, some sound that was always there. She pressed her arms to her sides in a shiver, and walked on. Why go back at all? He had to go back, but that was nothing to her.

Why make that long walk through the dark woods back to the gate, why not stay here in the ain country?

She had used to say that to herself, lying in bed in the high, still bedroom of the inn: Why not just stay here, never go back. . . . But she had never imagined what she would do if she stayed, how she could fit into the life of the town, which was complete without her. She came, needing help and willing to help, and learned to spin and card from the women, and went up to the Long Meadow with the children, and went down to Three Fountains with the traders, and made people laugh by her mistakes in speaking, and then left again. This was not her home; she had always called it her home, but she had no home; she stayed at the inn, there was no room here or anywhere that was hers.

She stood still under the iron gateway with her hands clenched.

"Irena."

She turned and saw him smiling at her.

"Come to my house," he said.

She went with him without speaking.

In the hall of the two hearths she stopped, and he stopped and turned to face her.

"Let me go north for you," she said. "To the City. Lord Horn won't send me. He'll send the man. Let me go for you."

As she spoke she saw the long roads across the twilit plain, the towers glimmering, the gates, the beautiful grey streets that went upward to the palace. She saw herself, the messenger, walk those streets. She did not believe it yet she saw it.

"With me," the Master said. "You will go with me."

She stared, utterly taken aback.

"The man leaves tonight. Tomorrow: meet me in the morning by Gahiar's yard."

"You can— We can go together?"

He gave one nod. His face was grim and set, but the incredulous blissfulness growing in her sang out O my master, my love, together!—but in silence; always in silence.

Sark walked on a few steps. "I shall be lord," he said very softly, his voice light and dry. "Not he, and not he, but I." He looked round at Irene with a curious smile. "Are you not afraid?" he said, with the old mockery.

She shook her head.

After early breakfast she left the inn; where the south road entered the street she turned left, passing Venno the carpenter's shop and old Geba's cottage. She strode along quickly, her stout shoes kicking her skirt aside so the striped stockings flashed. Her hands were closed and her lips set. The unpaved way ran beside the stonecutter's yard, deserted. She waited there, restless at first, pacing among the cedars and the blocks of roughcut stone, then sinking into a passivity of waiting, so that when she saw him come at last it was without relief and even without much understanding. Her feelings seemed detached from her mind and senses. She watched him come, a lithe, lean, dark man with a dark handsome face, and it was as if she had never seen him before and did not know him. He walked rapidly, rather stiffly, and did not halt as he came past the stonecutter's yard. He seemed not to look at her. "Come on," he said. She joined him on the road. He looked as usual, only that he wore a duffel coat and a sheathed knife or dagger on a loose belt, as the traders had done when they went down the mountain, but there was some change in him; he looked as he always looked but she did not know him.

The road turned a little. Now their backs were to the town, and to the threshold far behind. The way began to slope down into a cutting between high, reddish banks of earth.

"Come on!" he repeated. She had only slowed her pace to stay with him.

She went on a little way.

"Master," she said, turning. He had stopped. He stared at her. His eyes and face were very strange. He came on, walking directly towards her as if he were blind. She was afraid of him.

"Wait there," he said; his voice was thin and she saw that his jaw was trembling. "Wait. I—" He had stopped again. He looked around, his head shaking, looked up at the banks of the cutting, and past her at the road. He took one more step forward, and then with a whistling, whimpering cry tried to turn, his knees giving; he stumbled onto hands and knees and then lurching and staggering plunged back up the road. They had come no more than a hundred yards past the stonecutter's yard. She caught up with him there. "Master," she said, "don't, it's all right—" She tried to take his arm. He pushed her off with the blind strength of panic, throwing her right across the road, and ran on towards the town, making that thin, whistling cry.

She picked herself up, her head spinning a little and her forearm scraped on stone. She dusted her skirt, and stood dazed for a little while. She went slowly to a roughcut block of granite nearby and sat down on it, her arms pressed in against her belly and her head sunk between her shoulders. She felt a little sick, and kept wanting to urinate; at last she crept over to the ditch under the old cedars and squatted there. Up beside Geba's cottage the pair of scrawny goats blatted softly. She returned to the stone and stood staring down at it, the chisel marks and the patterns in the rock.

I wasn't afraid, she said to herself, but she did not know if that was true or false: his fear had so dominated and absorbed her.

He will never forgive me for seeing him like that, she thought, and knew that it was true, and could not bear the knowledge.

She left the stonecutter's yard, walking slowly past Geba's cottage and Venno's shop.

I could go, I could go on to the City, if it wasn't for him, she said to herself, vengefully, ragefully; but that she knew was false. Neither with him nor alone would she come to the City. It was all false, all lies and boasts and stupid daydreams. There was no way.

She stayed on only that one day and night more. She did not much want to stay at all, now. It was all spoilt, here. And she had left everything unsettled on the other side. She would get a place to live and so on and then she would come back here; maybe; if she felt like it. She was nobody's servant. She would do what she liked.

Her heart pounded as she set out on the south road, but it was fear of fear, nothing more; she walked on steadily. She did not look back. You don't look back, over your shoulder. She had learned that long ago, a child afraid of the dark, in the weird night aisles of the tree nursery, running. If you look back it will get you. In the city streets downtown, footsteps behind you and a long way to the next street crossing. You go on and you don't look back. The way down was steep and the woods very thick; she had never been so aware of the crowding of the trunks and mesh of branches. She tried to walk silently and then tried not to walk silently, for that was fear. At last she heard ahead the murmur of water, Third River, the stream at the foot of the mountain. It was beautiful, that sound of water running, the only music of the ain country. For you hardly saw the birds and they never sang, and the people of Tembreabrezi never sang, not even the children. The wind whispered or made its lonesome roaring in the high branches, but only the water sang aloud, for it rose from the places deeper than fear. She came to the stream, wide and shallow at the ford, gleaming and glancing under the old, moss-grown, leaning alders, quarreling cheerfully with every boulder in its course. She crossed, and then turned and knelt to drink. Now water ran between her and the mountain, and her heart was easier.

She was moving in the familiar half-trance of steady walking, the body alert and the mind occupied with thoughts so long and slow they cannot be put in words, for there are no words long enough, nor sentences, when her body carefully but without warning brought her to a halt, and only when she was standing stockstill, listening, did her mind ask, What was that?

The noise had been ahead of her. What she feared was behind her—but there! the white bulk lunging by the turn, ahead, there!—She held a branch she had picked up on the mountain for a walking stick—so she had called it to herself—and swung it up before her in a rage of terror and struck out. The blow was straight in his face but his arm was up as he broke through the thickets, and he took the blow on it. He stood, his head fallen back a little, his mouth open, his breath loud. His eyes were the eyes of the bull with a man's body in the narrow room. Her hand clutching the broken stick was numb. She took one step backwards on the path, a second, her eyes on him.

His gaping mouth shut, opened. "I can't," he said, thick and gasping, and shook his head. "Can't get out."

He sat down then, letting himself down heavily and shakily onto the weed-thick verge of the trail. He sat with his head bowed and arms lying on his knees, the heavy, simple posture of exhaustion. Her legs now were shaky with the aftermath of shock. She sat down crosslegged at a little distance from him, put down the broken stick, and rubbed her cramped right hand.

"You got lost?"

He nodded. His chest rose and fell. "Past the gate."

"You left town two days ago."

"The path kept going on."

"You stayed on it? Past the—where the gate should have been?"

"I thought it had to come out somewhere."

"You're crazy," she murmured, contemptuous, admiring the obstinate courage.

"It was stupid," he said in his hoarse, thick voice. "I finally turned around. But I thought I'd lost the path." He was mechanically rubbing the arm that had taken her blow. It was the white of his shirt she had seen in the thickets. Not very white close up, streaked with dirt and sweat.

She opened her belt pouch and got out the bread Sofir had given her—she had eaten all the cheese but only half the hard, dark bread at Third River—and handed it across the path.

He looked up; took it slowly; and ate it as she had never seen anyone eat bread: holding it in both hands and bringing his head forward to it, as if he were drinking or praying. It was very soon gone. He raised his head then and thanked her.

"Come on," she said, and he stood up at once. She felt the inward lurch and turn of pity, the body's blind compassion for the wound, seeing his heavy obedience and the white, weary face. "Let's go," she said as she would have said it to a child, and led off down the path.

After Middle River she asked him if he wanted to rest; he was late, he said; they went on.

They came down the last slope, across that beloved water, into the beginning place. She did not pause, for his fear drove her. She led on straight across the glade, between the high pine and the laurels, across the threshold.

At the top of the path in the heat and light of broad day and the sound of a jet dying off in the east and the reek of burning rubber from somewhere over the hill she stopped and let him catch up to her. "O.K.?" she asked with a little triumph.

"O.K.," he said. He was grey and wrinkled like a man of fifty, a bum with a two-day beard, a drunk or junkie, stooped and shaky.

"Oh, man," she said with awe, "you look terrible."

"Need something to eat," he said.

Since they had walked so far together they walked on farther together.

"You come every week?" she asked.

"Every morning."

That soaked into her for a while.

"You can always get in? The gate's always there?"

He nodded.

After a while she said, "I can always get out."

They came out of Pincus's woods. The light over the waste pastures was so bright it stopped them. A bank of smog lay translucent brown over the city westward. The sun burned through the haze with bleared, blinding radiance, all the air blurred with smog and burning with light. Each grass stem cast its shadow. The piercing rattle of a cicada swelled and died away and a bird called once, sharply, in the woods behind them. Their eyes stung, there was already sweat on their faces.

"Look," he said. "About your sign. I'm sorry. But I can't keep out."

"All right. I know."

She hunched her shoulders, staring out over the fields to the distant freeway. The running metal thread of cars flicked and stabbed the sunglare back. "It doesn't belong to me. Mostly I can't even get there any more."

They set off across the fields.

"I get here about five-thirty in the morning, usually," he said.

She kept silent.

"But I can't get to the town on the mountain and back before work. . . ." He was thinking aloud, slowly. "Next weekend. Labor Day. I get Sunday and Monday off. I can come then. They were—It seemed like they were asking me to come back."

"They were."

"O.K. So I could come then and stay a long time." He mumbled off into silence again, then said abruptly, "So if you want to."

After fifteen or twenty paces he said, "You helped me get out."

Irene cleared her throat and said, "O.K. When?"

"Six in the morning all right? Sunday."

"Fine."

As they came up the bank below the gravel road he turned right.

"My car's parked this way."

"O.K. So long then."

"Hey!"

He went shambling on.

"Hey, Hugh!"

He turned.

"You want a ride? You said you were late. Where do you live, anyway?"

"Kensington Heights."

"O.K."

As they walked toward the paint factory she said, "That must be a long walk from here. You don't have a car?"

"Rent on the crappy apartment costs too much," he said with sudden lucid violence.

"My stepfather'd sell you a car for fifty dollars."

"Yeah?"

"It'd run all week."

He didn't get the joke, such as it was. He was dumb with fatigue. In her car he sat hunched up in the deathseat. He was bigger than anybody who had ever ridden in the car with her, it was full of him. He smelled of dried sweat, rank fear-sweat. The hair on the backs of his big, white hands was brassy gold. His thighs were thick. She said nothing to him as she drove except to ask directions. She let him out at the sixplex apartment house he showed her, and drove away relieved to be rid of the crowding bulk and presence. She had not told him where she lived although they had driven past the farm. Did she live there? She didn't live anywhere else at the moment. For all she knew Rick and Patsi had made it up again by now, but screw them. Her mother wouldn't mind having her home again for a while, and it would be O.K. if she could just keep out of Vic's way so no trouble got started. She would be sleeping with Treese and that might discourage him. Or maybe not. But anyhow there was nowhere else to go until she found a place of her own. Maybe downtown. Did her mother need her nearby or was she just clinging to her mother? She ought to try. If only there was somebody who wanted to share an apartment downtown. At a stoplight she reached back to pick up and look at the alarm clock that lay on top of her stuff in the carton in the back seat. It was two-fifteen. She could go home and dump her stuff, and wash and eat something, and then start looking for an apartment. Maybe there would be something she could afford by herself. The Sunday papers were good for finding rentals, and there would still be time to go look at a place. Maybe she would find a place to live today, and not have to sleep at the farm at all, if she was lucky.

It was as if he had been blind and she had come to him, and his eyes had cleared to see her. Seeing her he saw the world, for the first time; there is no other way to see. Each act and object had its meaning, now, for when she had touched him her touch had taught him the language of life. Nothing was changed, but now it made sense. Apples three for twenty-nine and the canned snack pudding on sale eighty-nine for the first sixpack, all right, but that was the numbers and the words, and now he understood the equations, the grammar: the beauty of the world. The faces he had never seen before, because he had been afraid to look at the beauty of the world. People stood in line at his checkstand, restless and docile, obedient to hunger, their own hunger, their children's. Mortal creatures have to eat, so they were here, in the lines, pushing the wire baskets. So they would come to die. They were very fragile. They were spiteful, hateful when they were tired out and their money couldn't get them what they wanted or even what they needed; he felt their anger but it no longer angered or frightened him, for all things now contained the idea of her and were transfigured by it. The face of a little boy carried through the checkline by a tired mother, the dignity and patience of the little face and the heavy, unconscious grace of the mother's holding arm, made him want to cry out, as if he had cut or burned his hand. Things hurt. He had been numb. The anesthetic had worn off, he was alive, feeling pain. But within the pain, the reason for the pain, was joy. Beneath every word he said or heard, within everything he saw and did, lay her name, and around her name like a halo, an armor of light, the unshaken joy.

He looked at every blonde woman who came through the store. None had hair like hers, soft and pale, finely curled like a fleece, but he looked at them with tenderness and liking because they resembled her by so much at least, by being blonde. But there would be no woman like her, here. No woman here could speak her language. Her voice was clear and soft. His last day of the three days in the town on the mountain she had worn a green dress, a soft, narrow dress fitted to her round, slight body. Her wrists and neck were delicate and very white. In her all other women were beautiful, but there was none like her. There could not be, for she was alone, there, in the other land, where the soul became itself.

In books, men said that they could die for such and such a woman. He had always thought it made poetry but no sense, a mere habit of words. He understood it now as meaning exactly what it said. He felt in himself the longing, the yearning to give so greatly to the beloved that nothing was left, to give all, all. To protect and guard her, to serve her, to die for her—the thought was unendurably sweet; again he caught his breath as if a knife had gone into him, when that thought came to him.

"You haven't gone and joined that Swami Maha-Jiji or whatever it is, have you, Buck?"

He laughed.

"You got that sort of cross-eyed look they get, those hairy krisheners," Donna said.

She teased him in all sympathy, and he could not long resist her. He told her as much of the miracle as he could. "I met this girl," he said. Donna said, "I knew you did!"

101

with delight and satisfaction. But of course she wanted to know more, and he regretted having said even so much. It was wrong. He could not talk about anything from the evening land here. There was no way to say it. "I met this girl" was not true. The truth was that he had seen a princess, that he loved her, that he would give his life for her. How could Donna understand that?

She was kindhearted. She seemed to realise that he was unhappy at having said anything, and she stopped teasing him or even asking questions. But when she looked at him there was a glint in her eye, a cheerful twinkle of complicity. He did not want to see it. Donna was O.K., Donna was a very nice person, but how could anybody like that understand what had happened to him?—the strangeness, the mystery, the tragic fear; the fair, imperiled woman whom he loved in silence, the silence of worship, the silence of the unchanging twilight of the forests of that world.

This world of daylight and the night was strange enough, all that week. He had expected his impatience to return to the town on the mountain would make the waiting hard, but it was not so. Indeed, he savored and treasured these days when, at work or walking home or at home, he could cherish the thought of his princess and let her name fill his mind, instead of standing clumsy and tongue-tied in her presence, unable to speak to her and only guessing what she said.

He did not go the creek, the mornings of that week. He was afraid to risk the gate's being closed. He did not trust himself. Why had he been so stupid, going on across the threshold that had not been there, pushing on and on when he knew the way led nowhere? If, as soon as he saw the gateway was not open, he had headed straight back to Mountain Town and asked the girl to help him, he would have saved himself that nightmare, the endless walking, telling himself that if he just kept straight on he would "come out all right," and the panic that had taken him over when he thought he had lost his path, and the terror, and the hunger. It had all been stupid and unnecessary, and had left him not only so tired that he found workdays long and hard all week, but also distrustful of himself, or of the place.

"This is where I'm not afraid," he had said to the girl (in Allia's house, in the long room with the windows full of the clear twilight), but that was now no longer true. He knew now a little of the risk he might run in returning there. He knew also that he knew only a little of the risk. There was danger there; and he could not count on himself to act rationally. Given that, and the unreliability of the gateway, it seemed right to assess his chances of coming back as no more than equal. He saw this as part of the balance of the two places, and accepted it. It was the chance, the service he craved. But all the same, so long as he was here in the commonplace world, with the usual delusory options and nothing larger than life size to cope with, he would enjoy the light of day.

Towards his mother he felt the compunction, the grieving patience of potential disloyalty, strained only by her relentless crossness. She forgave him nothing. His coming back a couple of hours later than he had said he would on Sunday afternoon had brought bitter accusations of unreliability down on him. He understood that but did not understand why his unconcealable exhaustion (lamely explained by "getting lost on a shortcut") had aroused her antagonism and contempt. "You got lost in the woods? Why were you in the woods? If you don't know how to look after yourself it's a stupid, stupid, stupid thing to do. People like you should do their exercising in a gym. You haven't got the build for boy scouting. What are you trying to prove?" And so on: speaking from an uncontrollable irritation, it seemed, which made him think that it was not his coming back in such a state that enraged her, so much as his coming back at all. But that made no sense.

Lately she had been staying out three or four evenings a week, sometimes till midnight, at her séances with Durbina. Several other people with spiritualist interests had joined them. Mrs. Rogers had proved to have talent as a medium: she could do automatic writing without going into trance. Thanks to her gift, they were now carrying on a lively conversation, or correspondence, with one of Durbina's past incarnations, a priestess of Isis. The coffee table in the Rogers's living room was piled with books about ancient Egypt, borrowed from Durbina or, expensive as they were, bought new. When the priestess of Isis contradicted a statement in one of the books, or corrected an erroneous translation of a hieroglyph, Mrs. Rogers was triumphant. Sometimes when she got home she would talk excitedly about what had happened at the séance; but as soon as Hugh tried to respond she would come down from her high. "Of course, this sort of thing doesn't interest you," she said, no matter what he had said or asked. He saw that she was happy with these people who admired and valued her spiritualist talent, that she flourished among them. But she could not bring her ease or happiness home with her. Her new interests only increased her distrust and discontent. Hugh was unable to do anything to please her. If she did the laundry she complained savagely about odd socks, shirts with dirty collars and grass stains, T-shirts not turned right side out; but if he put the wash through she did it all over again because he hadn't done it right. If he brought something from the supermarket because it was on sale or a good buy, she said it was "day-old stuff," and let it molder in the refrigerator till he threw it out. When they were both in the apartment she made him feel that he was forever in her way, yet she said nothing to change her demand that he be there whenever she got home. If she stayed out half the evenings of the week, resented his presence yet insisted upon it, how were they going to manage, when he came back? . . . But the fact was, he was going. Against that fact his mother's non-negotiable demands became, at last, insignificant. Her rudeness and impatience hurt him, but not deeply; his will was turned aside from her. No knife's edge could reach him where he walked thinking of Allia.

It was hot, he said to himself, everybody got cross in weather this hot.

He moved through the long days of that week in silence, mostly. At night he had no sound sleep, but many dreams and wakings, and more than once in the small hours would get up to stand a while at the window to look up at the stars or the first high glory of the dawn.

On Friday Donna, who got Saturdays off, asked him what he was going to do over the holiday, and he answered, as he had planned, "Go hiking with some people I know." Donna gave him that sidelong flick of a glance that somehow implied that, in loving a woman, he had merited the approval of all womanhood as represented by Donna—or was it approval? But then she looked at him straight on, and her face changed. She put her hand on his arm. "Don't let anything happen to you, Buck," she said.

"What's going to happen to me hiking?"

"I don't know!" she said as if surprised at herself, and laughed it off.

But her look and words and the touch of her plump, hard hand with red-lacquered nails served him, in need, as a talisman, an assurance that in fact there was one person concerned about him, however ineffectually, through a mere intuition that he was in trouble or at risk.

If his mother's gift as a spiritualist led her to see the same thing she held it against him, as evidence of disloyalty, and did not forgive him for it.

On Friday evening he told her that he planned to be gone all Sunday night. This was what he had dreaded all week. He mumbled through the routine he had prepared about going hiking with some friends in the state park north of the city, taking the early bus on Sunday morning, sleeping out Sunday night, getting back on Monday afternoon. She said nothing. She kept her eyes on the television all the time he spoke, so that he could not be sure she heard. Though the live weight of guilt made it hard to breathe, he finished his statement, and then was silent, not asking, not permitting himself to ask, for confirmation, for permission, for the approval he craved, had always craved, had never got and would not get. But he would not permit himself anger either, and a while later, when her program was over and she had got up to turn the television off, he asked her as naturally as he could how her séance last night had gone. She did not answer. She took up a book on Akhenaton, and sat down with it, not looking at him or speaking to him. He tried to tell himself that her silence was easier to take than one of her tirades would have been; but as he sat in the room with her, trying to read *Time*, he found that he was beginning to shake, as if with cold. He got up and went to his room. She did not reply to his "Good night."

Usually she stayed abed on Saturday morning, but this day she was up and off in the car before Hugh got up. He went to work as usual. It was a heavy day, coming before the two-day holiday. She was not home when he got home. He ate supper alone. She came in at ten-thirty, looking thin, grim, a little disheveled in her cotton print dress. She did not answer his greeting but started straight down the hall to her bedroom.

"Mother," he said, and there was some authority of passion in his voice, for she stopped, though she did not turn to face him. The silence stood between them like a substance.

"There's no use you calling me that," she said in a clear, dry tone, and went into her room and shut the door.

Who can I call that? he thought, standing there. He felt as if something was being taken from him, out of his body;

106

he pressed his arms against his ribs to protect himself. There isn't anybody that there's any use calling father, he thought, and now there isn't anybody that there's any use calling mother. What a joke, I was born without parents. There isn't any use; she's right. And all that other stuff, the evening land, the town, Allia, that isn't real either. Kid stuff. But I'm not a kid. Kids have a father and a mother. I'm not, I don't. I haven't got anything and I'm not anything. He stood there in the hall knowing this to be the truth. It was at this time that he remembered, physically, with his body not his mind, the touch of Donna's hand on his arm, the color of her nail polish, the sound of her voice: "Don't let anything happen to you, Buck." He turned away from his mother's door then, went back into the kitchen and his own room to get ready what he would need tomorrow morning: the clothes he would wear, and a packet of bread, salami, and fruit for the long walk to the mountain.

He was awake at three, and again at four. He would have got up and gone, but there was no use starting early, since he had told the girl to meet him at the gate at six. He turned over and tried to sleep. The twilight of daybreak in the room, a shadowless dim clarity, was like the light of the other land. His alarm clock ticked by the head of the bed. He gazed at the whitish face, the hands both drawing downward. There were no clocks, there. There were no hours. It was not the river of time flowing that moved the clock's hands forward; their mechanism moved them. Seeing them move men said, Time is passing, passing, but they were fooled by the clocks they made. It is we who pass through time, Hugh thought. We walk. We follow beside the streams, the rivers; sometimes we may cross the stream. . . . He lay half-dreaming until five. As the silenced alarm clicked he stood up, feeling the floor cool on the soles of his feet. Within two minutes he was dressed and out of the house.

He was at the gateway before six. The girl was there waiting.

He was still not sure what her name was. When the people of the twilight said it, it sounded like Rayna or Dana; she had corrected him when he said Rayna, but he had not understood the correction. "The girl," he called her when he thought of her, and the word had about it a color of darkness and anger and the sound of the creek running. There she was standing near the blackberry thicket in the bluish, dusty, warm light of early morning under the thin-foliaged trees of the gateway woods. She looked up when she heard him coming. Her sallow face did not soften, but she held out her hand, palm up, purple-stained, offering him blackberries. "They're getting ripe," she said, and dumped them into his hand. They were small and sweet with the long heat of August.

"Did you try the gate?" he asked.

She picked a few more berries and joined him on the path, offering them to him. "It was shut." She went a little ahead and looked down the tunnel-like drop of the path among the bushes.

"It's there now."

"In again Finnegan, that's me," Hugh said, following. "Here goes." But he stopped on the threshold between the lands and turned, as he had never done before, to look back at the daylight: the dusty leaves, the sun-washed blue between the leaves, the flutter of a small brown bird from one branch to another. Then he turned and followed the girl into the dusk.

After he had knelt for his ceremonial first drink of the water of the creek, he saw that the girl had done the same thing. She was kneeling on the shelf-rock looking down at the running water, in no conventional posture of prayer or worship; but he knew from the hold and poise of her body that that water was, to her as it was to him, holy. She looked round presently, and stood up. They crossed the creek and went on into the evening land together. She went ahead, silent. The forest was entirely silent, once they had lost the voice of the water. No wind stirred the leaves.

After the broken, wakeful night Hugh felt thickheaded, content to walk forward through the forest wordlessly, mindlessly, following the steady pace the girl set. All thought and all emotion was in abeyance. He walked. He felt again that he could go on like this, striding easily under still trees, the cool air of the forest on his face, endlessly. He abandoned himself to the image without fear. When he had gone past the gateway, when he had lost himself, he had been terrified by that idea that he could go on and on and on under the trees in the twilight and there would never be any change or end; but now, following the axis, going the right way, he was entirely at peace. And he saw Allia at the end of the endless journey, like a star.

The girl had stopped and was waiting for him in the path, short solid figure, jeans and blue checked shirt, round grim face. "I'm hungry, you want to stop and eat?"

"Is it time?" he said vaguely.

"We're nearly to Third River."

"O.K."

"Did you bring anything?"

He could not get his mind in focus. Only after she had chosen a place to sit, near the path, beside a tributary streamlet that had been running parallel to their road, did he react to her question and offer to share his bread and meat. She had brought hard rolls, cheese, hardboiled eggs, and a sack of little tomatoes, rather squashed in transit but tempting in their bright innocent red, in this dim place where all colors were muted and no flower bloomed. He put his supplies beside hers; after he took a tomato from her side, she took a slice of salami from his; after which they shared freely. He ate a great deal more than she did, finding himself very hungry, but as he ate it faster they came out more or less even.

"Does the town on the mountain have a name?" he asked, feeling awake at last but much relaxed, and starting on the last piece of bread and salami.

She said a couple of words or a long word in the language of the land. "It just means Mountain Town. That's what I call it when I think in English."

"I guess I did too. What do you . . . You called the place something, once. The whole place." He gestured with his sandwich at all the trees, all the twilight, the rivers behind and ahead.

"I call it the ain country." Her eyes flashed at him, distrustful and defiant.

"Is that from their language?"

"No." Presently she said, unwilling, "It's from a song."

"What song?"

"There was this folk singer in assembly in school once and he sang it, it got stuck in my head. I couldn't even understand half of it, it's in Scotch or something. I don't even know what 'ain' means, I guess I thought it means 'own,' my own country." Her voice was savage with self-consciousness.

"Sing it," Hugh said very low.

"I don't know half the words," she said, and then, looking away from him and with her head bent down, she sang,

> When the flower is in the bud
> and the leaf is on the tree
> the lark will sing me home
> to my ain countrie.

Her voice was like a child's, like a bird's voice, sudden, clear, and sweet. The voice and the craving tune made the hair stand up on Hugh's head, made his eyes blur and a tremor of terror or delight shake his body. The girl had looked up at him, staring with eyes gone dark. He saw that he had reached out his hand towards her to stop her singing, and yet he did not want her to stop, he had never heard a song so sweet.

"It wasn't—it isn't right to sing here," she said in a whisper. She looked around, then back at him. "I never did before. I never thought. I used to dance. But I never sang— I knew—"

"It's all right," Hugh said, meaninglessly. "It'll be all right."

They were both motionless, listening to the tiny murmur of the stream and the immense silence of the forest, listening as if for a reply.

"I'm sorry, that was dumb," she murmured at last.

"It's O.K. We ought to go on, maybe."

She nodded.

He ate one more tomato for the road as they packed up their remnants. She went first again, which seemed right as she knew the way far better than he did. He followed her back to the axial path, the way she called the south road. Behind them and before them, to left and right, it was quiet, and the deep, clear light of evening never changed.

After they had crossed the last of the three creeks and begun the first steep climb, he found that he kept gaining on the girl instead of keeping about the same distance behind her. The quick pace she went had slowed, or become fitful.

At the crest of a foothill ridge from which, through a screen of thin, pale birches, the bulk and mass of the mountain loomed above and ahead, a darkness, she stopped. Arriving beside her in a couple of strides, Hugh said, "I could use a breather," for it had been a steep pull, and he thought she was tired and did not like to admit it.

She turned to him a drained face, a death's-head.

"You don't feel it?" He could scarcely hear her voice.

"Feel what?"

111

His heart had jumped, and was pounding uncomfortably.

She shook her head. She made a slight, hurried gesture towards the dark wall of the mountain.

"There's something ahead of us—?"

"Yes," she said, on the in-breath.

"Blocking our way?"

"I don't know." Her teeth chattered as she spoke. She was drawn together, hunched up like an old woman.

Hugh said aloud, "Listen, I want to get to the town." His anger was not against the girl but against her fear. "Let me go first."

"We can't go on."

"I have to go on."

She shook her head, despairing.

Determined to resist her reasonless panic, Hugh put his hand gently on her arm and began to say, "We can make it—" but she dodged from his touch as if his hand were hot iron, and her pinched face went dark with anger as she said aloud, "Don't ever touch me!"

"All right," he said with a flash of answering contempt. "I won't. Calm down. We have to go on. They're waiting for us. I said I'd come. Come on!"

He led off. To save his pride he did not look back to see if she was following; but he kept listening, down the long descent, for the light sound of her coming behind him. When the path went up again, he looked back for her. He knew what it was like to be afraid here. She kept fairly close behind him, and did not falter or hang back. Her face was closed like a fist under the black tangle of hair. In the high trees the wind made a sound like the sea heard from far off, the sea that lay far, far, far to the west, to the left, in the direction of the dark. Between the night and day they walked on the long path. It went on and on, and if she had not been coming behind he would have stopped. There was no end to the slope of the mountain, and he was getting tired. He had never felt so tired in his

112

life, a weakness all through his body, a languor that might have been pleasant if only he could sit down, could lie down, could stop and have rest. It was hard to go on, and it would be so much easier to go downhill.

"Hugh!"

He turned, and looked around bewildered for some time before he saw her. She was not behind him but above him on the slope, standing among dark firs. It was a dark place, the sky closed out by meeting branches and rocky slopes.

"This way," she whispered.

He realised that she was standing on the path. He had slanted off on a random track between trees, downhill.

The few steep paces back up to the path were a heavy labor.

"I'm getting tired," he said shakily.

"I know," she whispered. She looked as if she had been crying, her face puffed and blotchy. "Keep on the path."

"O.K. Come on."

At the end of the slope under the firs the way leveled out but was no easier, because the weariness kept growing, the heaviness, the longing to lie down. She came beside him now; there was room for them to walk together. When had the path become so wide, a road? She forced his pace now. He tried to keep up. It was not fair. He had not hurried her when she could not go on by herself.

"There—"

The gleam in the wide, cold evening: firelight, lamplight. Fear and tiredness were only shadows cast by that yellow gleam, shadows that fell behind them on the road.

They came into the town. There between the first houses they stopped.

The girl stood beside him, her weary, puffy face cocked back in defiance. "I'm going to the inn," she said.

He tried to shake off his dullness. Now that he was here where all his desire had tended he felt heavy, awkward, out of place. He had not the courage to go present himself at that great house, and did not know where else to go. "I guess I will too," he said.

"They're expecting you at the manor."

"The what?"

"The manor. Isn't that what they call where a lord lives? Lord Horn's house. Where you were last time."

Her tone was sharp and jeering. Why did she turn against him after the hard way they had come together? She was unreliable, not to be trusted. She liked to see him make a fool of himself. Well, that was a wish easily granted.

"So long," he said, and turned towards the first side street that led up the hill.

"One street farther down. The one with the steps," the girl said, and went on towards the peak-gabled, bow-windowed, galleon-like bulk of the inn.

He followed, passed the inn, turned left up the many-stepped street. The air smelled of woodsmoke like all autumn in a breath; a child's voice called far off where the town below ran out into pale pastures. There was a strange noise in the low-fenced yard by the top house of the street: geese hissing, Hugh realised when he saw the big, white-shouldered birds eying him. There were birds and beasts here in the town, there were voices, but still no voice sang. The geese hissed and shifted. Although he had come where he desired to come he was tired and cold, a chill not from wind or weather but from within, from the marrow of the bone and the dark pit of the bowels, a hollow, weary coldness.

He passed under the iron gateway and between the lawns and came to the high house, its roofs dark against the evening sky, two windows throwing a soft light across the walk. He lifted the knocker in the shape of a ram's head, and knocked.

The old servant opened the door, and he heard his own name pronounced as they said it here, foreign, all one word, spoken with energy and welcome. The old man hurried before him through the unlit galleries, and opening the door to a crimson-walled, firelit room, announced him joyously by that same splendid half-familiar name: "Hiuradjas!"

Allia was there in the glowing room. She rose, dropping some handwork, and came forward, her hands held out to him. Her light hair was lifted by the lift and turn of her body. There is no way to expect beauty, or to deserve it. He took her hands. He could have fallen at her feet. He did not know her language but her voice said, "You are welcome, welcome, welcome! You have come back at last!"

He said, "Allia," and she smiled again.

She asked him something. The look of her blue eyes and the tone of her voice were so gentle in their concern that he said, "It was hard coming, it was frightening—I got tired—" But he saw from her gesture now that she was only asking him if he would sit down, which he did, gratefully. Then he was up again because Lord Horn had come in, greeting him with cordiality and with something else which Hugh did not recognise at first: respect. This man, elderly, called "Lord," clearly used to personal authority, showed towards him not deference, not mere politeness, but the regard of equality: as if they were of the same family. As if Horn spoke to some quality in him which he did not know himself, but which the old man knew and greeted.

Allia's friendliness, though shy and mannerly, was much less sober than her father's. All conversation they could have was a kind of running language lesson. She happily performed the necessary pointing and handwaving and facemaking, and laughed at her misunderstandings and at his mistakes. Yet in her too he sensed an attitude towards him which he did not want to call respect but dared not call love; the most he could admit to himself was that she seemed to like him, to admire him—what for? What had he done? Nothing. How could she value him for what he was? Equally nothing. Yet in her soft, frank look and voice and even in her laughter at his blunders there was the underlying grave temper of admiration. Such admiration as he felt for her: but it was her due. All she was and did was admirable and beautiful. If he was to be admired it was only by a kind advance. Nothing was due him. But to earn, to deserve what she gave him undeserved, to be the man she mistook him for, he would do anything.

They dined in a candlelit, long room. He was so tired that the meal passed in a blur of light and warmth. When he was alone in his room he felt drunk with weariness. The bedroom, where he had slept the three nights of his first stay here, surprised him by its deep familiarity: the walls painted in faded blue and almost-rubbed-off gold, the oak bedstead, the brass-capped andirons, were as pleasant to recognise as if he had known them all his life. Though in no way like it, the room recalled to him a room he had carried in his mind for many years, an attic in the first house he had lived in, his father's mother's house. His bed had been by the window that looked out on the dark green fields and blue hills of Georgia. That was another country and a long time ago. Here the high windows were curtained. A fire burned, bright and almost soundless, in the small fireplace. The bed was high and hard, the sheets cold, heavy, silky to the touch. In that bed, the gold eye of the fire gleaming between half-closed lashes, there were no dreams. There was only sleep, the wide, drifting darkness of sleep. As he gave himself up to that all thoughts, distinctions of light, impulses of will slipped away from him; only for a moment he heard above the darkness a thin voice like a bird,

When the flower . . .

He turned over and buried his head in his arms, driving the song away, deeper down, into the source. It had no place here, where no flower came into bud, and no leaf fell, and no voice sang. But Allia was here, holding out her hands to him as he went gladly into darkness.

116

6

Why did I come back?—The question presented itself insistently, irritably, like a child whining. She turned on it with exasperation: Because I had to! And now she had to do what had to be done next. She went to the house at the top of the street of steps, and Fimol let her in, and in the beautiful room between the hearths she waited, so tense and apprehensive that all she saw and heard was uncannily vivid, disjointed, a primitive bright meaninglessness.

The Master came into the room. Not as she had seen him last, hunched in terror, whimpering, unseeing. None of that. Straight, alert, calm, and grim: the Master. "Welcome, Irena," he said, and as always she was tongue-tied, unable to resist his ascendancy, and welcoming it with relief. This is how he truly is, I can forget that other face. He is my Master!

But on the other side of that awkward and passionate submission, as if through a pane of glass, a cold soul stood watching him and herself. That soul did not serve; nor did it judge. It watched. It watched her choose the stiff brocaded chair to sit in and wonder why she chose it. It watched him pace down the room, and saw that he was glad to have his back to her.

The fires were not lighted. The air of the long room was

tranquil, like the air inside the lip of a thin-walled sea shell.

"Soon now we shall have to begin to slaughter the sheep," the Master said. "There's no forage left at all in the eastern low meadows." The low meadows were the pastures close to town, normally used only in lambing season. "But since the salt traders haven't come, we won't be able to preserve much of the meat. A great feast; the feast of fear . . ."

The people of Tembreabrezi did not tend their flocks for meat but for wool; their wealth was the fine wool they dyed and spun and wove, and traded for what they needed from the plains. "The King's cloak is of our weaving," Irene had heard them say.

"Is there nothing you can do?" she asked, appalled by the idea of them killing their pride and livelihood, those flocks of beautiful, canny, patient beasts. She had been up on the mountain with the shepherds many times; she had held newborn lambs in her arms.

"No," he said in his dry voice, his back to her, standing at the windows that looked on the terraced gardens of his house.

She bit her lip, because her question had hit the center of his shame. She had seen, seen with her eyes, that there was nothing he could do.

"There are things we could have done. The animals knew first. We should have heeded them. The wild goats came by—the sheep would not go up to the High Step; all that we saw. We knew, but still did nothing. I was not alone in saying there were those things that must be done. There were men who said it before I did. That we must take the price and make the bargain. But the old women cried, oh, no, no, this is not to be done, this is disgusting and needless. All the old women, the Lord of the Mountain among them. . . ."

He had turned to face her. The light was behind him so she could not see his features. His voice was dry and reckless.

"So we took the counsel of the cowardly. And now we

118

are all cowards. And all helpless. Instead of one lamb, all our flocks. No child of our own, but this boy, this stupid boy who cannot speak our tongue. He is to set us free! Lord Horn was a wise man, once, but it was long ago. If only I had gone to the City when I dreamed of it first. But I waited in deference to him. . . ."

His last words meant nothing to her. Little of what he said made sense, but his vindictiveness had broken her habit of timidity. She asked without hesitation, "What do you mean? How is the stranger to set you free?" When he did not reply she insisted: "What is he to do?"

"To go up on the mountain."

"And do what?"

"What he came to do. So says Lord Horn."

"But he doesn't know what he's here for. He thinks you know. He doesn't know anything. Even I felt the fear, coming, but he didn't."

"A hero is indifferent to fear," the Master said, jeering. He came a little closer to her.

"What is it that we fear?" she said steadily, though now she was afraid of him. "You must tell me what it is."

"I cannot tell you, Irenadja."

His face was dark, congested, his eyes bright. He smiled. "You see that picture," he said, and she glanced for a moment where he pointed, at the portrait of the scowling man. "He was my grandfather's father. He was Master of Tembreabrezi, as I am. In his day the fear came. He did not listen to the old women whimpering, but went out, went up to make the bargain, with the price in his hand. And he struck the bargain, and the ways were freed. He came down the mountain alone, and his hand was withered as you see it there. They say it was burned away. But my grandfather, who was a child then, said it was cold to the touch, cold as rotten wood in winter. But he paid the price for all!"

"What price?" Irene demanded, fierce with fear and revulsion. "What did he hold—what did he touch?"

119

"What he loved."

"I don't understand."

"You have never understood. Who are you to understand us?"

"I have loved you," she said.

"Would you do as he did, for love of us? Would you go there, to the flat stone, and wait?"

"I would do anything I could. Tell me what to do!"

His eyes burned now. He came so close to her that she felt the heat of his face.

"Go with him," he said in a whisper. "The stranger. Horn will send him. Go with him. Take him to the High Step, to the stone, the flat stone. You know the way. You can go with him."

"And then?"

"Let him make the bargain."

"With whom? What bargain?"

"I cannot tell you," he said, and the dark face burned and writhed. "I do not know. You say you have loved us. If you have loved me, go with him."

She could not speak, but she nodded.

"You will save us, Irena," he whispered. He turned his face as if to kiss her, but the touch of his lips was dry, feathery, hot, less touch than breath.

"Let me go," she said.

He drew away from her.

She could not speak and did not want to look at him. She turned and walked the length of the long room to the door. He did not follow her.

She did not return to the inn, or go to see Trijiat. She went down the steep streets alone, and out the east end of town past Venno's shop and Geba's cottage, to the stoneyard. There she sat on the granite block, and on the wall by the road, and crumbled the little, elegant cones of the cedars in her hand, and thought; but it was not so much thinking as a long grieving, which she must grieve through as a musician plays a tune through, from beginning to end. Often her eyes were on the road north, the road that led down to the City, the road she could not go.

She was summoned the next day to the manor. She wore her red dress and her second-best stockings. Palizot tried to lend her a new pair, and her thin-soled shoes, "to be proper at the Lord's house," but Irene refused and went off dogged and sorehearted, in the same dull, grieving mood under which lay, like the deep cold water under the reeds of a sea marsh, fear.

She did not look up towards the peak as she went from the iron gateway to the manor house.

As before, the old manservant took her to the windowed gallery, and the same people were there. This time they had got Hugh Rogers dressed up like themselves. She wished she had worn her jeans and shirt in defiance, and at the same time wished she had worn the thin shoes and striped stockings. She eyed his finery: narrow black trousers, heavy shirt of linen, long vest worked with dark embroidery. He looked well in it. He was heavy but well proportioned; his throat was white and massive in the high, open collar, he carried his head erect. He came forward eagerly to her and spoke to her with clumsy good will. He was happy in his fine clothes, with the old man patting him on the back, and the old man's daughter simpering at him, and all the food and attention and friendship heart could desire, sure, and then out you go to do what can't be done and thanks a lot; it's what you came for, isn't it?

The Master was there, talking with old Hobim and a couple of other townsmen. She did not once look directly at him, but was continually aware of him, and at the sound of his voice her heart stopped and waited.

Lord Horn's daughter stood with Hugh. She was talking to him now, teaching him a word, the "adja" they tacked onto the end of your name when they wanted to call you friend, trying to explain that his name as they heard it, Hiuradjas, already had the word in it and would sound ridiculous if they added it, Hiuradjadja! and she laughed saying it, a soft, merry laugh. He stood staring at her porcelain face and sheepswool hair. Fool! Irene thought. Stupid fool! Can't you see? But she saw the softening of his mouth, the stillness of his eyes, and she was awed.

"Alliadja," he said, and went red, face and ears and neck red under the thick, fair, sweaty hair; and then white again.

Allia smiled, sweet and cool as water, and praised him.

"They could be sister and brother," said a voice speaking near Irene—speaking to her, she realised, startled from the absorbed compassion with which she had been watching Hugh.

Lord Horn had come to stand by her. He was not looking at her but at Allia and Hugh, set apart by their blondness from the others there. The old man's long face was severe and calm as always. Irene said nothing, taken aback by the curious irony or intimacy of his remark. Presently he turned to her. "Will you be long with us, this time, Irenadja?"

"Only as long as I can be useful," she said with sarcasm. Then she was ashamed. It was Horn who had said to her, "Your courage is beyond praise," words she had treasured against frustration and self-doubt. There in the other land, where she could find no home, she had not thought who had said them to her, but had held fast to them: your courage, you have courage. . . . You will not force your mother to make the choice she cannot make; you will not ask for help she cannot give. You don't need help. Your courage is beyond praise.

"Lord Horn," she said, "I wish I had gone to the City, when—when people still could go."

"There is more than one road to the City," he said.

"Were you ever there?"

He looked at her with his grey, distant gaze.

"I have been to the City. That is why I am called lord, because I have been there," he said, kind and cold and calm.

"Did you see the King?"

"The shadow," Horn said, "I saw the bright shadow of the King," but the word was feminine so that it must mean the Queen or the Mother; and none of the words he spoke meant anything, and she understood them as she had never understood anything in her life. His eyes that looked always from a distance were on hers. If I reach out my hand and touch him I will see clearly, she thought. The screen will be gone and I will stand both there and here. But in that knowledge I am destroyed.

Horn's grey eyes said gently, Do not touch me, child.

Someone was approaching them where they stood beside the hearth. She turned away slowly from Horn and saw, with indifference, that it was Master Sark.

"Now that Irena is here, my lord, we can speak to your guest more freely," the Master said, deferent yet officious, impatient.

The old man looked at him and spoke as always after a pause: "Very well. Will you speak for us and for him, Irena?"

"Yes," she said. She felt released from the stupor that had bound her down so long. She felt she could trust her own will again. She caught Hugh's attention; the other people, falling silent, gathered round the hearth in a loose half-circle. Allia stood nearest Hugh. He looked from her to Irene with alert, clear eyes, a little apprehensive, candid as a child. Lord Horn spoke, and Irene translated his words and Hugh's.

"We are asking your service, we are asking your help."

Hugh nodded.

"We have no claim on you. If you do what we ask it is in pure mercy to those who have no other hope."

"I understand."

"We cannot help you, and you will be in danger."

After a moment Hugh said, "What is the danger?"

She did not understand all Horn's reply, but put it into English as well as she could: "We who live here are afraid—are the fear, he said—and so cannot face the enemy—only the other, the stranger, can turn its face, his face—I don't understand what he's saying, really."

"Ask him who the enemy is."

She asked. Horn answered, "The eye that sees gives form; the mind that knows, names." So his words came out in English as she spoke them.

"Riddles," Hugh said with a smile. He thought it over, began to ask a question, and checked himself; he waited. Patience became him, Irene thought. There was dignity in him, under the clumsiness. Part of the clumsiness, perhaps.

"What will you give him to take, my lord?" the Master said.

"The sword I was given, if he wants it," Horn replied.

"What will you give him to give, my lord?"

She had begun to translate this for Hugh when she realised that the old man was speaking, slowly as ever, but with harsh weight: "You are your grandfather's grandson, Sark, but where are the children of his daughter?"

"All of us," the dark man said. "All of us are her children."

"The children of fear. And so we are bound. And our right hands useless. Would you sell us again, Sark? Allia, bring the sword."

She crossed the room to a chest against the inner wall, and knelt, and opened the lid.

The tension between Horn and the Master was so great, and its sources so obscure to Irene, that she did not try

124

to interpret their exchange to Hugh. She and he both stood watching Allia.

Her pale fleece of hair floating, the girl returned across the room carrying on her hands a bright, thin strip of light. She stopped before her father; he motioned briefly and gravely towards Hugh. She turned to Hugh and raised her hands a little; she was smiling, but her lips and face were pale.

Hugh looked at the sword, and said under his breath, "My God."

Without looking up from it at Allia or Horn or Irene, he took hold of the grip, awkwardly and with a dogged expression on his face, and lifted the sword from the girl's hands. It was evidently heavy. He did not raise it or try to test or flourish it, but held it clumsily across the air in front of him, like a barrier.

"I judge from this," he said with detachment, "that whatever it is I have to face is real."

"I guess it is," Irene whispered.

"I was hoping it would be magic. It would be easier. Listen. You'd better tell them that I didn't take fencing in high school."

He set the point of the sword down carefully on the polished floor and stood with his hand on the pommel, looking down at the handle and blade with an expression of grudging respect. The beautifully modeled grip looked right for his big hand; the blade was very thin and long. The hilt, where Irene looked for a crosspiece as in a picture-book sword, was a massive oval flange set with a ring of yellow stones.

Looking up from the sword at last, she saw that she was the first of them to do so. Sark's face was pinched and aged; Horn gazed imperturbable.

"He says he has no skill with swords, my lord," Irene said, and felt a strange small pleasure of malice in doing so, a solidarity, against Horn and all of them, with Hugh.

"I do not know if any skill would serve him," the old man said. "I could not send him out unarmed." His voice was sad, and the spark of defiance died down in Irene.

"It's his sword, from the City, I think," she said to Hugh.

"Thank you," Hugh said to the old man, in the language of the twilight; and to Irene, "Well, can they tell me where to go, and what to do?"

When she asked his question, several of the men who had stood silent, listening, replied: "On the mountain," one said, and another said, "In the mountain," and old Hobim said, "It is the mountain." The Master took the word from them. "Up the mountain, in the summer pasture on the High Step. Irena knows the way there."

"No!" Allia broke in, her face gone wild and terrified. "Let me go—I will go with him—"

"You cannot," Sark said. "You will be crawling on hands and knees, begging to turn back, before you have crossed the bridge." He spoke with vindictive satisfaction, not trying to conceal it. Allia turned to her father, with her hands up over her white face, weeping.

"Tell me what they say," Hugh said to Irene, desperately.

"They want you to go up the mountain, to the highest meadow. Allia wants to show you the way, but she knows she can't. Lord Horn—"

But the old man was speaking, to Sark: "You would send the child, again, Sark? You know only the one way. But you can no longer send her, or keep her. And a road goes two ways. Where are their faces set, who came to us from the south?"

"Tell them never mind," Hugh said. "I'll go where they say. If I go out looking for trouble with this thing, I expect I'll find it."

"It's a long way and there are different paths. I'll go with you, I've been up there."

"All right," he said, unquestioning.

126

She turned to Horn. "He will go. I will go with him."

The old man bowed his head.

"When shall we go?"

"When you will."

"When do you want to go?" she asked Hugh. She was beginning to feel shaky; Allia's tears made her want to cry.

"The sooner the better."

"You think so?"

"Want to get it over with," he said with simplicity. He looked at Allia, who stood protected by her father's arm; she did not look up to meet his eyes.

"Tomorrow," he said, after a little pause. "Ask them if that's O.K."

"You're the boss."

"What's wrong?"

"I don't know. Why can't they say— It isn't fair. For all I know they're just sending you out as a—I don't know. A scapegoat. A—" But she could not think of the word she wanted, that meant something given up as an offering.

"They're stuck," he said. "They can't do what they have to do. If I can, then I will. It's all right."

"I don't think you ought to go."

"It's what I came for," he said. He looked at her, completely unselfconscious. "What about you, though? If you think it's a mug's game . . . No use both of us being stupid."

She saw the firelight run in long slivers of tawny red up the blade of the sword.

"I know the way, you'll need somebody. But anyhow. I don't want to stay here. Any more."

"I could stay here forever," he said under his breath, looking at Allia, not at her face but at the white hand against the blue-green dress.

"Most likely you will," Irene said, but an unwilling pity muted her bitterness, her sense of betraying and having been betrayed; and he did not understand her.

127

She was asked to stay and dine with them at the manor, but excused herself and got away as soon as she could. Hugh didn't need an interpreter; he got on better without speaking the language than she did speaking it. And she could not bear to be with them any longer. It was her fault, she had been a fool, but it was too late now. It was all too late. She had paid no heed to the wise and dangerous man, and had made her promise to the empty-hearted one. She had mistaken herself, and chosen to be a slave. So she was left now to look at her master, her mirror, and see no trust, no honesty, no courage. His darkness was emptiness, and all he felt was envy.

And yet, if Allia were to look at him, would she not see that proud man Irene had seen? It was they that belonged together, he dark and bright, she fair and cool. How could he not be envious when Hugh stood beside her? Sister and brother, Lord Horn had said looking at Hugh and Allia, but looking at Allia and Sark he would say lover and lover, man and wife. And that was as it should be. All here was as it should be, as it must be; all but her, who did not belong here, or anywhere, having no house, no people of her own.

She ate supper with Palizot and Sofir, and spent a little while in the firelit kitchen with Palizot after supper, but there was no going back to the old tranquillity. The thread on which she had strung her life was tied off; the game was done. She had pretended to be their daughter but it had never been the truth, and now the pretense was only a constraint upon affection. And, knowing she was going up on the mountain in the morning, though they tried not to show it they were in awe of her. Sofir was miserable. Palizot carried it off better, but the hypocrisy was trying to all three of them, and Irene soon bade them good night and went to her room.

She drew the curtains across the changeless clarity of the sky, lighted the fire, and sat down to think. No thoughts worth thinking came. She was weary. She went to bed. There, before she slept, listening to the wind which was gusting a little, buffeting the dormers of the old house, she thought, "Whatever happens, I won't come back to Tembreabrezi. It's time to go. To be gone. He only made me promise to do what I would have done anyway." There was no comfort in the thought, yet it quieted her. Resentment, the sense of betrayal, rose from resisting the knowledge that she must go, pretending she could keep what she had loved. There was nothing to keep, except maybe the willingness to love. If she lost that she was lost, all right.

She asked herself why she was no longer afraid. Her tiredness now was the memory in nerve and muscle of the endless sickening fear she had felt coming, this time; but though she made herself imagine going out on the road, going up on the mountain, no awful chill began in the pit of her stomach, no panic in pulse or mind. Maybe that meant she had finally made the right choice—done what you came for, as Hugh said, poor Hugh, heavy and anxious, with his honest eyes. He was going though he did not want to go, wanted to stay. What choice was right, then? But that would prove itself, and meanwhile there was no fear, but only sleep, here rising from the sources deeper than dream, beyond the screen of word or touching hand, the mountain that is within the mountain, the sea that is in the spring, here where no rain fell.

When the household woke and she got up, she dressed in her jeans and shirt and desert boots, intending, as always when she left the ain country, to take nothing across the threshold with her; but then she went to the chest in the hall for an old, patched cloak that Palizot had given her when she went down the north road with the merchants. It was of dark red wool, much stained, ragged at the hem, but warm, and easily carried as a little back roll. Sofir, with the same idea that this journey might not be over with in a day, had made her a hefty packet of dried meat and cheese and hard bread, enough for several days certainly, and she rolled that up in the cloak.

She and Palizot clung to each other for a minute. Neither could say anything. It was an end, and words are for beginnings. She kissed Sofir and he kissed her, and she left the inn.

As she came out into the courtyard she saw Aduvan and Virti and other children, waiting for her, looking excited but a little frightened or bewildered. They did not say much, but clustered around her as if for reassurance. A group of people were coming down the street of steps: Horn and Allia, Sark and Fimol, a group of old men and women, and Hugh amongst them, tall and white-faced, the ox led to slaughter. They waited at the foot of the street and Irene with her escort of children came to join them.

Other people stood in their doorways along the street that led westward through town. They greeted Lord Horn softly by his title, and Hugh and herself by name. "Irena, Irenadja." Some joined their group, and others gathered at the crossings. She realised that this was their parade. Sad and quiet the people of Tembreabrezi gathered to honor them, to wish them well, to send their hope with them.

A young father held his baby up to see Hugh go by. That made her want to laugh, a foolish, jeering laugh, and she scowled to prevent the laugh. Big Hugh, in the handsome leather coat they had given him, and his backpack, and the sword in a leather sheath at his side, would have looked like a hero if only he had known he was a hero; but he looked wretched, embarrassed, hunching his shoulders and losing his share in glory because nobody had ever told him he had a share in glory.

The street leading west out of town became a road, pavement stones giving way to packed earth. The houses on either hand were lower, and then fewer, and then the fields began, walled with rock, and the long low pastures where all the flocks were now, west and north of town. People had joined them so that as they walked between the walled fields there were forty or fifty walking along together, easily and quietly. With a leap of the heart Irene thought, "Maybe they're coming with us, maybe all they needed was to start out with us, and we can all keep together and go on." But the parents of the children were walking with the children, now. They had taken the children's hands; they stooped to them and spoke softly. No voice spoke aloud. "Irena," Aduvan said in an unhappy whisper, standing beside her mother and little brother. Irene turned back to them. Other children put up their arms to her, whispering, "Goodbye!" Virti would not kiss her; he cried, whimpering, "I don't want to see the bad thing, I don't want to see it!" Trijiat turned back with him. Irene went on; she looked back once; the children stood there on the road, in the dusk. No lights showed behind them in the town.

Women and men stopped, one by one. They stood still on the road, watching the others go on. The soft, restless wind blew by them.

The shoulder-high wall of dryset stones continued on the left, and on the right a high hedge darkened the way. She could just make out the whitish stones of the bridge that carried the mountain road over a small torrent which spread out below as a stream watering the pastures. That would be the boundary: the bridge.

"Goodbye, Irena," a woman said softly as she came past. The wind blew out her grey skirt a little, her face looked pale in the dim light on the road. She was Aduvan's grandmother, Trijiat's mother; she had taught Irene to spin. "Goodbye," Irene said to her. The road curved a little to the left, towards the bridge. She passed the Master standing rigid and desperate, his hands clenched at his sides. She said, "Goodbye, Sark," calling him by his name for the first time and the last. He did not or could not speak. She went on a little farther and halted beside Lord Horn. Near him, Allia's hair shimmered in the dusk of the road as if it held light in it, as she stood facing Hugh.

"May our hope go with you, may our trust support you," Allia said in her soft, clear voice in her own language. He said only, and only Irene understood it, "I love you."

"Farewell!" Allia said, and he repeated the word.

Lord Horn's hand, thin and light, was on Irene's shoulder. She looked up at him startled. Smiling, he kissed her on the forehead. "Go without looking back, my daughter," he said.

She stood bewildered.

Hugh was going on towards the bridge. She must go with him. She passed Allia, standing silent in the dark road like a statue. He called me daughter, her heart said, he called me daughter. She went on. They all stood silent in the dusk on the road behind her. She did not look back.

The road crossed the bridge and curved further left, west, beginning to go up onto the mountain. Thick trees on one hand now, the high hedge on the other. It was dark on this road.

Hugh kept a swinging pace, a little ahead of her and to her right; she saw him as a bulk and movement in twilight.

The hedgerow had given place to forest. Dark branches met overhead. The road was walled and roofed by tree-trunks, branches, leaves. A tunnel. Glimpses of sky between the branches. The heavy, ferny odor of the forest. Something huge, pallid loomed by the road ahead. As Irene's heart lurched, her mind said, It's the boulder, calm down, it's only the boulder by the high trail. Already? Yes, already, it's been a long time since we left the town, since we crossed the bridge, a couple of miles. "Hugh," she said.

Only now, speaking, though she spoke barely above a whisper, did she hear the silence. The wind had died. Nothing moved. It was like deafness. There was no sound.

Hugh had stopped and turned to her.

"This way," she whispered, pointing left. She could not make herself speak louder. "The trail up to the high meadows."

He nodded, and followed her as she turned off the roadway onto the narrower, steeper track, worn deep by the hooves of the flocks, that led up into the mountain.

Her heart continued to beat hard, her ears to sing. It was the climbing, she told herself, but it wasn't that. It was the silence. If only something would make some sound, something besides her own walking and her breathing and the faint drum-drum-drum in her ears, and Hugh coming along behind her, not making very much noise, but any noise was too much here.

I will not be afraid, I will not be afraid. Just keep on going the way you have to go. Just don't get lost like a fool.

It had been a couple of years since she had been on this path. She had used to come with the shepherds and the children and the flocks, following. Now she must find the way alone. She kept questioning it, but there was no mistaking: look at the path, she told herself, it's the sheep path, that's dried sheepshit there, there's the marks their hooves make, this is the right way. I will not be afraid.

Brush had begun to encroach across the trail since it had gone unused. It was not a hard trail but it took ceaseless alertness, and was all uphill. Abruptly, at the top of a sharp pull, they came out of the forest darkness. The air seemed almost bright. There was a clear view of land and sky. They had come out at one end of the Long Meadow, an immense alpine pasture, a terrace in the northeast face of the mountain.

She stood under the last trees, in the high grass, getting her breath after the climb. Hugh stood beside her. She saw his chest rise and fall in deep, even breaths as he looked along the distances of the meadow and the slopes that rose sheer above it.

"Is this the place?" he asked.

It was the first word he had spoken since they crossed the bridge.

"No. About halfway I guess. The High Step is on up there." She pointed to grey cliffs and crags overhanging the Long Meadow far to the right of where they stood. "With the sheep it took two days to get up there; they always camped here in the Long Meadow."

"I wondered why they gave me all this food."

"Saint George and the sandwiches," Irene said, and a fit of crazy laughter came over her and went away as fast as it had come. She looked at Hugh. He had slipped off his backpack and leather coat and was readjusting his belt, scowling. "Damned sword keeps tripping me." He looked up and met her eyes. "It's all fake," he said, and turned red. "Playacting."

"I know."

But the silence hung around their voices, and they heard it.

"You don't feel the—" he hesitated, with clumsy delicacy—"the fear?"

"Not exactly. I feel nervous, but not . . . I feel like it had its back turned."

He got the sword slung to his satisfaction, ran his hand through his hair, and sighed, a big *houf!* sigh.

"You never have felt it?" she asked with curiosity.

"I don't think so."

"That's good."

"Last time, when I went past the gate, I was scared. You know. Really scared, panicked. But that was because I was afraid of getting lost. It isn't like that, is it?"

She shook her head. "Not at all. It's more like you're going to find something you don't want to find."

He grimaced.

"It's awful," she said. "But I've never been afraid of getting lost, here. I always know where the gateway is. And the town. And the city, I guess."

He nodded. "It's all on the same line, the same axis. But when I went past the gate I lost that. It all looked alike. I didn't even recognise the gateway creek when I crossed it. If I hadn't met you—"

"But you were on the path—almost on it. It's more like you panicked and didn't think."

"When they said I had to go up the mountain, off the axis, I was about ready to panic again. When you said you'd come, that made . . . You know. Like I had a chance."

He was trying to thank her, but she did not know how to be thanked.

"What did you mean about playacting?"

"I don't know." He stood looking out across the meadow. Miles of high, flowerless grass, silvery green in the unchanging light, bowed very slightly to the wind. The sky was empty. No bird, no wisp of cloud. "The sword, I guess."

"You think you won't need it?"

"Need it?" He looked at her rather stupidly.

"What's it for? What is it you're supposed to fight with it?"

"I don't know."

"What if you aren't even supposed to fight—it isn't any good? If there is something up here, some sort of creature or power or something, why don't they tell us what it is? What if there's no use trying to fight it?"

"Why would they trick us?" he asked, his voice grave.

"Because it's all they can do. I don't mean Lord Horn is bad. I don't know what he is. You can't say good and bad about what they do. Like you said, they do what they have to. The Master talked about making the bargain, about paying. He meant—I don't know what he meant. I just don't understand it, I don't know what we're trying to do here."

Again he ran his hand through his thick, sweaty hair. "But you didn't have to come up here," he said in his gentle, obstinate way.

"Yes, I did. I don't know. I had to. It was time to go."

"But why this way? You could have just gone home."

"Home!" she said.

He did not reply for a while. He nodded once. "I guess so," he said. And after a moment, "Let's go on. I keep thinking it's going to get dark soon."

7

The grass was high, thick, tangled, showing no path. The girl set off confidently, angling towards the grey crags far across the great terrace of grass. There was no need to go single file here, as on the narrow forest trails. Hugh kept alongside her, but a couple of yards away, for she had left no doubt that she disliked to be crowded or even approached. The dense, lithe grasses tangled his feet, and he learned to set his foot straight down at each stride, as when walking in snow. The clumsy sword banged at his thigh, but it was pleasant to get a rhythmic stride going, instead of groping and climbing. And it was a pleasant and rare thing in this forest land to have their goal in sight, to watch the crags slowly towering higher.

After a long time he spoke. "Now I keep thinking it's morning."

The girl nodded. "Because it's lighter up here, I guess. No trees."

"And open to the east."

They walked on steadily, silent. In this vast, empty grass-land it seemed natural that there should be no sound but the faint lash and flick of the grass against their legs, and sometimes the hum of wind in the ears. A mild exultation came into Hugh's body and mind, a buoyant rhythm in time with his stride. He was doing what he had come to do, going where he had to go. He had earned his right to be here, his right to love Allia.

It did not matter that she did not know the language in which he had said, "I love you." It did not matter if they never met again. It was his love that mattered, that bore him onward, without grief or fear. He could not be afraid. Death is love's sister, the sister with the shadowed face.

As they went on and slowly the cliff towered higher and the folds and scars and slides of its surface revealed themselves, and the wild grass lashed and flicked in the rhythm of his stride, and the depths of the sky lay overhead like water, he felt once more that he would be content to walk in silence across the high land forever. There was no weariness in him now. He would never grow tired. He could go on forever, his back to everything.

The girl was saying his name. She had said it more than once. He did not want to stop. There wasn't anything worth stopping for. But her voice sounded thin, like the voice of a sea bird crying, and he stopped and turned back.

Some while ago they had come directly under the cliffs, and had since been walking northward in shorter grass beside huge falls and slides of broken rock half overgrown with broom and grasses. The girl stood a good way behind him, at the outer fold of a cleft in the base of the cliffs, which he saw as he came back to be the entrance to a path. It looked a dark, narrow way.

"This is the way up to the High Step," she said.

He looked at it with disfavor.

"I want a break before we start up. It's steep," she said. She sat down in the grass, here dry and short, tawny, worn-looking. "Are you hungry?"

"Not very." He did not want to bother with eating, though when he thought back he knew they had come a long way and walked a long time, that the dark road where Allia had stood was very far behind, below, down there.

He wanted to go on. But the girl was right to stop, and she looked tired, her face pinched and frowning. He dropped his coat and swordbelt and sword and pack near her and went off behind a waste of huge fallen boulders to piss; came back, feeling with pleasure the warmth and spring of his whole body, untired but glad now to rest a little; and levered himself up onto a reddish boulder beside the girl sitting in the grass. She was eating. She passed a strip of dried meat and some chips of some kind of dried fruit to him; and it tasted good.

There was one sound: the wind whistling in the dry grass or past the tumbled stones, a tiny, cold piping, low to the ground.

She wrapped up the packet of food.

"Better?" he asked.

"Yes," she said, and sighed. He saw her round, sallow face turn towards the dark path.

"Listen," he said. He wanted to say her name. "You don't need to go on."

She shrugged. She stood up, fastening her homemade backpack, a roll of red wool.

"The place I'm supposed to go is at the top of that path?"

She nodded.

"O.K. No problem."

She stood with her sullen look and then, startling him, she looked at him and smiled. "You'd get lost," she said. "You keep getting lost. You need a navigator."

"I can't get lost on a path two feet wide—"

"You did, when we came, you walked right off the south road." The smile broadened to a laugh, very brief. "When I get scared, you get lost. Seems to be how it works."

"Are you scared now?"

"A little," she said. "It's starting again." But the laugh was not altogether gone.

"Then you shouldn't go on. It's not necessary. I feel responsible. If it wasn't for me you wouldn't do it."

But she had started up the path. He followed her at once, shrugging his pack on hurriedly. They entered the cleft, a raw vertical scar in the mountain wall. High, dry walls of red and blackish-brown rock closed in upon them. The way was stony, and immediately steep.

"You're not responsible for what I do," she said over her shoulder.

"Then you're not responsible for keeping me from getting lost."

"But we have to get there," she said.

They climbed on. The path turned sharply back and forth. There was a scramble up, where rocks had slipped. Hugh looked at the girl's hand as she steadied herself against a raw-edged boulder. It was a small hand, thin and dark, the crescent moons of the nails white.

"Listen," he said. "I want to—I never did understand your name."

She looked back at him. "Irena," she said clearly, and spelled it.

He repeated it, and again the broad, sweet, secret smile went across her face as she looked down at him, steadying herself among the harsh ruin of raw earth and rock. Then she went on, going lightly.

The sword impeded him constantly here, the heavy leather scabbard either tripping him or whacking his thigh or driving like a crutch up under his arm; he finally got it riding secure at the right angle on the swordbelt, but in doing so fell back a long way behind the girl. As he went on he heard a sound of water running. He turned one of the numberless sharp elbows of the path and saw a small stream scurrying transparent across the way from its spring in the rocks, dropping down into a basin of green weeds and ferns. Irena was kneeling by it waiting for him to catch up; her face and hands were wet and muddy. He knelt too and drank, his hands sinking into the miniature bog beside the rivulet. The water tasted of iron or brass, like blood, but very cold.

The way was always narrow, always steep, following the fissures in the wall of stone. Where there was dust underfoot it was marked, dried mud scored, with the narrow hoof-prints of the last flock that had been driven down the mountain. The strip of sky overhead stood high and remote. Not much light came down to the path except where it followed the side of a widening canyon for a while. When the walls narrowed in again Hugh felt that it was leading into, inside the mountain. His hiking boots slipped on the stone; his footing was uneasy. He envied the girl, who went like a shadow up the steep, twisting way ahead of him.

She stopped at the foot of a long straight stretch. He caught up with her and asked, whispering because of the deep silence, "You all right?"

"Just winded." Like him, she was breathing hard.

"How long does it go on?"

The rocks overhanging the path were strangely shaped, bulbous, as if waterworn long ago. They looked like half-formed animals, tumors, huge entrails of stone.

"I don't know. It took all day with the sheep."

Her eyes, in this rock-weighted dusk, looked dark and frightened.

"Go slower," he said. "There's no hurry."

"I want to get out of here."

Twisting and burrowing in the gorges, the path went mercilessly upward. Twice again they stopped to get their wind back. The last stretch was so steep that they clambered as on a ladder, using their hands. When abruptly the way leveled and there were no more walls, Hugh was on all fours. He stood up and then, his head swimming, dropped back to his knees. The cleft path had ended on the outer edge of a second alpine meadow, narrow, a green shelf. A thousand, two thousand feet below, the great meadow they had come from lay distance-misted, green as moss. He had no idea how to judge the height, the miles; but they were high up, for the enormous slant of the mountainside was now perceptible, both above this meadow and below it, as the main direction of this part of the earth, as absolute as the horizon, which itself lay so high and far that it was lost in the thickness of the twilit atmosphere. Overhead and north and east from the mountain arched the calm, unimpeded sky.

Irena was sitting in the grass, nearer the edge than he wanted to be. She was looking northward over the lower lands. Hugh looked to the east: down the slopes at first, wondering if from here you could see the gleam of the lights of Mountain Town, but it made him dizzy again to look down. He looked out, across the gulf of air, to the eastern mountains. Behind those dim outlines, as if drawn with grey pencil on grey paper, was there a hint of color, of brightening? He watched a long time, but could not be sure. When he followed Irena's gaze to the north he saw no glimpse of the lights of towns, no faint clustering brightness that might be the City far away. All was blue-grey, indistinct, silent, vast.

She stood up finally and moved inward from the edge, walking carefully. "This is the High Step," she said, half whispering. "My legs are all rubber from climbing."

It made his head swim to see her stand between him and that immensity of empty air. He got up and faced inward towards the meadow. Across the grass—short, up here, and vivid, like a lawn—between the edge and the mountain wall rising above, there was an outcropping of rock, a kind of island in the grass. He walked towards that. It was a mass of big, licheny, grey rocks, tumbled and cracked, reassuring in size and solidity in this high, strange place. It felt good to get the rock at your back. They both sat down there with their backs against the main rock mass, fifteen or twenty feet high.

"That was a long pull," he said. She only nodded. He got food out of his backpack and they shared it in silence. She leaned her head back against the rock and closed her eyes. The profile of her face was small and stern, like a bronze coin, against the sky.

"Irena."

"What?"

"If you want to go to sleep I'll watch out."

"O.K.," she said, and without more ado curled down against the rock with her red backroll for a pillow.

He ate another dry roll—hard, knot-shaped, grainy, with a pleasant taste—and a lump of goatsmilk cheese, which he did not like but was hungry enough to eat; after consideration, he ate one more roll stuffed with a strip of smoked mutton, and then put the food back into his pack. He wanted more but this would do. He felt a great deal better for it. It was a long time and a long way since they had left the town, and he was tired, but not worn out. Only if he sat here with his back comfortably against the rock he would fall asleep, like her. He ought to keep watch. He got up and began a leisurely patrol back and forth by the rock island.

In the clarity of this high-altitude light, less a dusk than a translucence, an everywhereness of light without source, the color of the grass was intense: dark and clear like an emerald. The forests closing off both ends of the shelf-meadow—nearby to the south, distant to the north—looked rough and black. Above the cliffs that overhung the meadow, the next riser of these huge stairs, hung the same rough blackness of trees, steep and remote; above that, bare rock, the summits. In this world of air and rock and forest there was no color but the dark jewel green. No flowers bloomed in the alpine grass. No flowers could open in the grass when no stars opened in the sky. This seemed clear to Hugh; then he decided his mind was getting fuzzy. To wake himself up he changed his patrol, going part way around the rock island; not all the way. He did not like to leave the sleeping girl out of sight.

Around the north end, in towards the cliffs, there was a bald place in the grass. The second time he came to that end of his semicircular route he went closer to see why the ground was bare there. It was not ground but stone, a shieldlike expanse of rock, a shoulderblade of the mountain showing through the skin. The slightly swelling surface was broken at several places; he came closer to look. Iron rings were bolted into the stone, four of them, making a rectangle several feet long. Rust had stained the stone and lichen-scurf around the sockets of the bolts. He stepped up onto the flat rock and tugged at one of the rings, but it held firm. A strip of rawhide thong knotted around it and broken off at the knot had shrunk onto the metal till it seemed an excrescence of it. They were ugly, the thick, rust-scaled rings fastened to the rock, between cliff and gulf, an ugly place. The girl was sleeping there beyond the boulders on the open side, defenseless. That was wrong. He was wrong to be here. This was the wrong place. He turned his back on the flat stone and as he did so he heard the crying in the forest.

A crying, a distant, hissing, sobbing noise, hardly louder than the sudden pounding of his heartbeat.

He ran. The sense of the abyss of air beyond the edge swam in his head. The girl slept; he shook her, saying, "Wake up, wake up."

"What is it?" she muttered, confused, scowling, and then her eyes went wide as she heard the voice, already much louder, nearer, howling and sobbing in the forests at the north end of the meadow.

"Come on," he said, hauling her to her feet. She grabbed her bedroll and came, gasping and silent. He did not let go her arm, for at first she could hardly move, weak with sleep or terror. He pulled her along with him for a few steps, then suddenly with a spasm of release she shook off his hand and began to run. They headed for the forest at the near end of the meadow, running away from the voice. Neither had made any conscious decision. They ran. The voice loudened behind them, a sobbing howl beating and beating in their ears. They reached the forest that had offered a hiding place and now loomed a maze, a labyrinth of dark paths where they would be lost. "Wait!" Hugh tried to shout to the girl, but the breath burned in his lungs and he had no voice, and she could not hear, for the monstrous desolate howling filled the world. She stumbled and swerved from a tree trunk and ran up against Hugh, grabbing at him blindly, her mouth open in a strange square shape. She pulled him off the path they had been following. He plunged with her downhill between tree trunks and thickets, leaf and branch lashing face and eyes. The ground steepened, slipped underfoot, they stumbled and slid down the slope fifty feet or more to fetch up against the bulwark of a half-rotten fallen tree where, the breath knocked out of them, paralysed, they cowered. The voice beat all thought from the mind, louder yet, horrible and desolate, enormous, craving. Hugh looked up and the creature from which the voice came was there, on the path above them, the thickets shaking and tossing as it came and passed, white, wrinkled, twice a man's height, dragging its bulk painfully and with terrible quickness, round mouth open in the hissing howl of hunger and insatiable pain, and blind.

It passed. It was past, dragging the hideous sound behind it.

Hugh lay with his shoulders against the fallen tree, struggling to breathe, to get air into his lungs. The world slipped and whitened around him. When it began to steady, when the pain in his chest lessened, he became aware of warmth and weight pressed against him, against his left side and arm. "Irena," he said in a voiceless whisper, giving that warmth a name, pulling himself back with the name, the presence. She was crouching doubled up, her face hidden. "It's all right," he said.

"It's gone," she said, "it's gone."

145

"Is it gone?"

"It went on."

"Don't cry."

She had sat up but her warmth was still next to him, and he turned his face against her shoulder, in tears.

"It's all right, Hugh. It's all right now."

After a long time his breath came evenly again. He raised his head, and sat up. Irena drew away a little and tried to comb the leaves and dirt out of her hair with her fingers, and rubbed her wet cheeks.

"What now?" she said in a little, husky voice.

"I don't know. Are you O.K.?"

Neither had been hurt in their plunge down the hillside, though the cuts where branches had whipped Irena's face showed like red pen lines. But Hugh felt beaten, weary, with that deathly weariness which had come over him on the road from the gateway; and Irena seemed to share it, sitting with eyes half closed, her head bent down.

"I can't go any farther now," she said.

"Neither can I. But we ought to get out of sight." It was an effort even to speak.

They crawled and slid on hands and knees a few yards farther down the increasingly steep slope. A big stand of rhododendrons had made a niche for its roots, a kind of nook. Under the high old bushes the leafmold was deep, with a soft, bitter smell. Irena slid down into that niche, and sitting there hunched together like a child began to unstrap her woolen pack, which she had clutched under her left arm the whole time. Hugh crawled on a little way under the bushes till he could stretch out face down. He wanted to unbuckle his belt to get free of the sword, but was too tired. He put his head down on his arm.

146

She was sitting with her legs stretched out, under the outer branches of the rhododendrons. She looked round when she heard him moving. He levered himself down beside her, and hunched his shoulders to shake the stiffness out. He had slept so heavily his body was still soft with sleep, he could hardly close his hand. The lines on Irena's face were black now, ink scratches, but it was no longer the skull-face of terror and exhaustion; it was round, soft, sad.

"Are you O.K.?"

She nodded.

"I wonder if there's a stream down there," she said after a little.

He was thirsty too. Neither felt like eating any of the dry food in her pack until they could drink. But neither moved to go seek water. This nook, walled and sheltered by the dark old bushes, seemed protected, protecting. They had found refuge here. It was hard to leave it.

"I don't know what to do," Hugh said.

Both spoke softly, not whispering but under their breath. The mountain forest was quiet, but not dead still; some faint motion of wind broke the hush.

"I know," she said, meaning she did not know either.

After a while he said, "Do you want to go back?"

"Back?"

"To the town."

"No."

"I don't either. But I can't— What else is there to do?"

She said nothing.

"I have to take the damned sword back to them. And tell them."

"Tell them what?"

"That I can't do it." He rubbed his hands over his face, feeling the sore, stiff growth of beard on jaw and lip. "That when I saw it I fell down and cried," he said.

"Come on," she said fiercely, stammering. "What could you do? Nobody could. What do they expect?"

"Courage."

"That's stupid. You saw it!"

"Yes." He looked at her. He wanted to ask her what she had seen, for he could neither forget nor believe the image in his own eyes. But he could not bring himself to speak directly of the thing.

"It would be stupid to try to face it," she said. "It wouldn't be courage, just stupid." Her voice was thin. "When I even think of it I get sick."

After a pause, his voice sticking in his throat, he said, "Is it—did it have eyes?"

"Eyes?" She pondered. "I didn't see."

"If it was blind . . . It acted blind. The way it ran."

"Maybe."

"You could be ready for it. If it's blind."

"Ready!" she mocked.

"It's the noise. The damned noise it makes," he said in despair.

"That's the fear," she said. "I mean it's like that's what happens when you feel the fear—you're hearing that voice. I heard it once when I was asleep. It's like it just turns your mind off. It's just— I can't do anything, Hugh. I can't be any help. If it comes again I'll just run again. Or not even be able to run."

Not even be able to run: the words stood in his mind. He saw the flat stone in the grass. The iron rings in the stone. The knot of rawhide through the ring. His breath stuck and cold saliva welled into his dry mouth.

"What did they say to do?" he said. "They said a lot you didn't translate. They gave me the sword, they sent us up here, to that meadow—"

"Lord Horn didn't say anything. Sark said to go to the flat stone. I guess he meant that pile of rocks we sat down by."

"No," Hugh said; but he did not explain.

"I guess they just knew that if we went there we'd—it would come—" She was silent a while and then said very quietly, "Bait."

He said nothing.

"I loved them," she said. "For so long. I thought . . ."

"They were doing what they had to do. And we—we didn't come here by accident."

"We came here running away."

"Yes. But we came here. We got here."

This time she did not reply.

After a while he said, "I feel like I ought to be here. Even now. But you've done what you promised. You ought to go on now, go on back down to the gateway."

"Alone?"

"I couldn't protect you if I was with you."

"That's not the point!"

"It's just dangerous for you here. I don't need you, now. If I was alone, I could—I'd be able to act freely."

"I already said you're not responsible for me."

"I can't help it. Two people are always sort of responsible for each other."

She sat silent, hugging her knees. When she spoke it was without defiance. "Hugh. What could you do better alone? Except get killed?"

"I don't know," he said.

Presently she said, "We ought to eat something," and crawled back under the rhododendrons for her bedroll. She laid out the packets of food and sat looking at them.

"My pack's back by those rocks," he said.

"I don't want to go back there!"

"No. This is enough."

"Well, it could be a couple of days' worth. If we stretch it."

"It's enough." It did not matter. Nothing mattered. He was defeated. He had run away and hid, again, and he was safe and always would be safe and never free. "Let's go," he said. "I'm not hungry."

"Go where?"

"Down to the gate. And get out of here."

She looked up at him as he stood up. Her face was un-happy, indecisive. He refastened the swordbelt, settled the leather coat on his shoulders. His muscles ached, he felt ill and heavy. "Let's go," he repeated.

She rolled up her red pack and strapped it, keeping out a strip of dried mutton, which she held in her teeth as she slipped her arms into the straps. He set off, climbing the steep, thickly forested slope they had descended, until he came to the path that entered the forest from the High Step. On it he turned left.

Catching up to him with a considerable racket of rustling leaves and cracking twigs, Irena said, "Where are you going?"

"To the gate." He pointed, with certainty, a little left of the direction of the path. "It's down there."

"Yes. But this path—"

He knew she meant but did not want to say that it was the path the white crying thing had used, had made.

"It goes the right direction. When it stops going the right direction we'll cut across country to the axis path, the south road."

She did not argue. She looked worried still, but there was no use worrying, it did not matter how they went or where. He went on, and she followed.

The trail was faint but quite clear, without side trails or deer crossings to confuse the way. It went fairly level, and the direction was south, though it wound left and right in u and v curves as it followed the hollows and musculature of the mountainside. The trees grew thin-trunked, close, and high. Often there were rock formations, outcrops of pale granite, and occasionally a bare rocky slope above the path. Where the earth was softer under the trees the fallen

150

fir needles were swept off the path in places and the dirt was scraped aside and scored. Noticing that, Hugh thought of the heavy, pumping, pale, wrinkled legs, the dragging body. It ran upright, as a man runs. But it was much larger than a man, and ran heavily but very quickly, dragging itself and crying as if in pain. Once allowed into his mind the image was with him constantly. He thought there was an odor in the air along the path, vaguely familiar, no, intimately familiar, but he could not name it. There were white flowers in summer on some kind of bush that smelled like that, like semen, that was it, the sweet, dull smell. He went on and on and had nothing in his mind but the endless moment of the glimpse of the white thing running above him on this path.

A small stream crossed the way, rising from springs higher on the mountain. He stopped to drink, for he was very thirsty. The girl came up beside him. He had forgotten for a long time that she was there, behind him, coming along. The gleam of the water and the shape of her face came between him and the image of the white thing. After drinking, Irena washed her face, washing off dirt, salt, blood, sluicing the water up her arms and on the back of her neck. He imitated her, and the touch of the water roused him a little, though his mind worked slowly and everything seemed dull and dim, without meaning or difference.

She was saying something.

"I don't know," he said at random.

For a moment he saw her eyes, dark and bright in the formless twilight under the trees.

"If we're still on the east side of the mountain, then that's south," she said, pointing. He nodded. "The gateway. But the path turns so much. I'm getting mixed up. If we're going to leave this path we should do it now, maybe, while I still have some sense of the—of where the gate is." Again she looked at him.

"We should stay on the path," he said.

"You're sure?" she asked with relief.

He nodded, and stood up. He crossed the little stream, and they went on. It was dark under the close, dark trees. There were no distances, there was no choice, there was no time. They went on. The trail descended gradually now. All its turns veered farther to the right than to the left as it led them around the mighty contour of the mountain westward. It will get darker as we go farther west, Hugh thought.

Irena pulled at his arm: she wanted him to stop. He stopped. She wanted him to sit down and share food with her. He was not hungry and could not stay there long, but it was pleasant to rest a little while. He got up, and they went on. Steep streams crossed the path now and then in the dark infolds of the canyons, and Hugh knelt to drink at each, for he was always thirsty, and the water roused him for a minute. He would look up and see the sky between the black jagged branches, and look beside him at the quiet, soft, severe face of the girl kneeling next to him at the stream's edge; he would hear the sough of wind above and below them on the mountainside. He would be aware of these things, and perhaps of the small ferns and water plants beside his hands. Then he would get up and go on walking.

There was a place where the air was lighter, a stand of some round-leafed, pale-trunked trees. There the trail forked. One branch turned, going left and downhill; one went straight on.

"That one might go down to the south road," Irena said, but he knew from her saying "that one" that it was not the right one.

"We should stay on this one."

"It keeps going on. We must be going west by now. Maybe it just goes around the mountain and comes back out at the High Step. It just goes on and on."

"It's all right," he said.

152

"I'm tired, Hugh."

It was no time since, it was a long time since they had stopped to rest or eat. He wanted to go on, but he sat down and waited there at the fork of the trail under the pale trees while she ate. They went on. When they came to a stream, they drank, and went on.

The way went uphill now. Those were the only directions: right and left, uphill and downhill. The sense of the axis was long since lost, meaningless. There was no gate. The trail became very steep, zigzagging in and out of the ravines that scored the mountain's bulk, always uphill.

"Hugh!"

The name he hated came from a great distance in the silence. The wind had ceased to blow. There was no sound anywhere. Be quiet, he thought with a dull stirring of anxiety, you must be quiet now. He stopped walking, unwillingly, and turned around. He did not see the girl at all for a while. She was far down the path behind him, down the long, dim, steep path under the crowding trees, her face a white patch. If he had gone on a few steps more they would have been out of sight of each other. That would be better. But he stood and waited. She came very slowly, she toiled up the slope, that was a word from books, toiling, working, it was hard work to walk this road. She was tired. He felt no tiredness, only when he stopped and had to stand still, as now, that was hard. If he could go on he could go on forever.

"You can't just keep going," she said in a breathless, harsh whisper when at last she had come up to him.

It was a great effort for him to speak. "It's not much farther," he said.

"What's not?"

Don't talk, he wanted to tell her. He managed to whisper it, "Don't talk." He turned to go on.

"Hugh, wait!"

The anguish of fear was in her whispered cry. He turned

back to her. He did not know what to say to her. "It's all right," he said. "You wait here a while."

"No," she said, staring at him. "Not if you're going on." She started past him up the narrow trail with a kind of plunge forward, walking with a jerky, driven gait. He came behind her. The path turned, and climbed, and turned, under the dark firs, under the rock faces. They went round a corner that jutted out over immense, dim, dropping forests, and saw all the evening land beneath them darkening into the distant west. They did not pause but went on, entering under trees, into leaf and branch, into the mountain, under rock. To the right the walls of the summit buckled, overhanging. The trees among the scarred crags and boulders grew short and sere. There was rock underfoot now, and the path went level.

Irena's heavy, jerky pace faltered. She stopped. She took a few steps and stopped again. As he came up beside her she whispered, "There."

They faced a cliff wall, around which the trail passed on the outside, narrowing. Hugh went those few steps more, and turning the corner saw the inner curve of the cliff, a rock face overhung by half-leafless bushes. In the rock was the mouth of a cave. There it was, of course; this was the place. He stood gazing at it without fear or any emotion. He was here. At last. Again. He had been coming here all his life and had never left it in the beginning.

It only remained to walk the few steps down to the stony level ground before the cave, and go in. In the cave it was dark. Not twilight: darkness. From the beginning of time until the end.

He started forward.

She ran past him, the girl, pushing past him on the narrow path, running down and across the stony level to the cave mouth, but she did not enter. She stooped and picked up a stone and flung it straight into the dark mouth, screaming in a thin voice like a bird, "All right then, come out! Come out! Come out!"

"Get back," Hugh said, coming beside her in three strides. Holding the sheath with his left hand he drew the sword with his right, for there was no other help. The cold breath sighed out of the cave, and from the cold dark, wakened, came the huge voice, the gobbling howl. And the face that was no face, slit and eyeless, was lunging out, thrusting blind and white, groping down upon him. Holding the sword grip in both hands Hugh pushed the sword upward into the white, wrinkled belly and dragged the blade down with all his strength. The whistling sob rose into a scream. In a gush of pale blood and glistening intestines the creature reared up writhing, pulling the sword out of his hands, and then crashed down on him, crushing him as he tried, too late, to throw himself aside into the clear.

8

It still moved. The jerking of the arms—small, like a lizard's forelegs, against the mass of the body, but shaped like human arms and hands—was rhythmic, a reflex without intent. Human arms, a woman's arms, and those were breasts, pointed like a sow's teats, between the arms and lower down the belly, there where, as the pulsing spasm of the body went on, the wound was brought into view again, and again, and again, and the grip of the sword protruding from the wound. Irena, on hands and knees, crouched down lower and vomited on the rocks and dust. When she could raise herself up a little she began to crawl away, to get away from the dying creature and the reek of the opened belly. But Hugh was lying there under the thing and how could she leave him there? But he was dead too or dying and she was frightened, there was nothing she could do. She could not even stand up. She kept trembling and making a queer noise like "Ao, ao." When she had crawled up close, under the twitching arms, so close that she could see the entrails sliding inside the wound, and Hugh on his back pinned under the huge wrinkled leg and body, she could not even get hold of him. She could not tug him out. She had to move the dragon thing, to try to push it off him. When she set her hands against the white wrinkled side she screamed aloud.

It was cold, a dead coldness. It was inert and stiff, the spasms running through it mechanically. She pushed, her head down and her eyes shut, weeping. It moved a little, rolled under her push, rolled slowly over onto its back, freeing Hugh's body lying in a gush of slime and blood. The thin white forearms were now raised up into the air. Their twitching, fainter and faster, was in the corner of Irena's vision as she crouched beside Hugh. He lay on his back, both legs bent to the side, his face masked, effaced with blood. She tried to clean the stuff off his face with her hands, to get his nostrils and mouth clear, for he was breathing, a gasping shallow breath at intervals; but he lay motionless and his face felt cold. The dragon thing had fallen on him and lain on him too long, chilled and stifled his life. He was broken. If she could get him out of this mess, the blood and the burst intestines and the white shuddering bulk she would not look at, if she could just get him somewhere else and get him clean and make a fire and get warm, both of them get warm. But she could not move him. If his back was injured she could kill him trying. She did not dare even move his legs, afraid they were broken.

"What shall I do?" she whimpered aloud, and felt her tongue dry and swollen in her mouth. She had been thirsty for a long time, for miles before they came to the cave, for hours while Hugh went on at that remorseless steady pace, never stopping, driven or drawn, and she could only stay with him because she knew that neither of them would ever get out of this country alone. And the way had gone higher and higher, and there had been no more streams, and they had come to the cave. But her mouth was like dry plaster, and there must be water somewhere. She sat back on her heels, looking with half-seeing eyes about the stony level in front of the dark gap of the cave mouth, the bare slopes and cliffs above, the treetops and rising ridges across the gorge. She would not look at the white thing, but the tremor of the forearms was always at the edge of her eye; it had almost ceased, a running shudder. She tried to wipe her hands on stones, for they were sticky and growing stiff with slime and blood. She heard the breath catch in Hugh's throat. He moved his hands and coughed, a small, thin sound like a child. His lips worked, and presently he opened his eyes. There was no mind in them at first, but as she crouched beside him and said his name he looked at her, she saw his blue eyes, his soul alive.

"Can you move, Hugh? Can you sit up?"

The breath whistled in his chest.

"Wind 'ck'd out," he said very faintly.

"It's all right. You got knocked down. If you can move, we'll be able to get a ways away. I can't move you."

"Fat," he said. "Wait."

He shut his eyes, then presently opened them, set his lips, and got himself propped up on both elbows, his head hanging over his chest. "Hang on," he said to her or to himself. "That's it," she told him, holding his shoulder, "that's the way." He got up onto his knees with a lurch. There he stayed for a while. He showed no awareness of where he was, did not see the dead thing shivering beside him; he could go no further than his own body now. When he tried to stand up, Irena could help him, getting her shoulder under his arm as a crutch. He was very heavy, shambling, not seeing. She guided him in a staggering shuffle around the body of the dragon creature, across the level, into the thin trees that grew beside the cave wall. The trail went on there. Almost at once it turned sharply left and downward, descending so steeply that Hugh could not keep his feet. At least they had got past the cave. She was going to have him sit or lie down there on the trail while she went to find water, when she heard the sound of water running; and she thought then that all along she had heard that sound, while they were in the stony place in front of the cave. She got Hugh to shuffle on around the turn

158

of the path. The trail ran down among high ferns. Above it water slipped in a clear film over boulders, crossed it, and vanished among ferns and moss down the mountain-side. "Here," she said. As soon as she ceased to support him Hugh went down onto his knees again, and then onto all fours. "Lie down," she said, and he let himself slip down on his side among the ferns.

She drank and washed her hands and face in the little ceaseless, clear rilling, and gave Hugh water in her hands, a swallow at a time, the best she could do. She tried to get him to sit up so she could get his coat off. He did not cooperate. "It's all covered with blood and, and tripe, Hugh, it smells—"

"I'm cold," he said.

"I've got a blanket, a cloak. It's dry, you'll be warmer."

His resistance was not conscious, and by persisting she got the leather coat off him. He cried out twice with pain as she tried to work it off his shoulders, so that she thought his shoulder was broken or dislocated, or his arm injured; but he said clearly enough, "It's O.K." All the front of his shirt was sticky, pale brownish-red; she got that off him too. She could see no injury on him. His shoulders, arms, and chest were heavy, smooth, and strong, very white in the dusk place among the ferns. She got him wrapped in the red cloak, and when she had washed out his shirt she used it to clean his face and throat and hands better; then rinsed it again, craving and healed by the water, the touch and cool and clarity of it. When she let him be, he lay with his eyes closed. His breathing was still shallow, but quiet. She sat with her hand on his, for his comfort and her own.

The immense gorge they overlooked was still. All the mountain was still, except for the small constant music of the spring.

It was a good place, this nook beside the path: the ferns, the boulders, the film and glimmer of water, the steady dark branches of the firs. She looked up. The path had turned sharp round; they must be directly below the stony level and the cave mouth. The spring must rise beneath the floor of the cave. It came out here into the light. They were in front of the cave here, but on beyond it, past it. You never think of going on past the dragon, Irena thought. You only think about getting to it. But what happens afterwards?

She began to cry again, noiselessly, painlessly. The tears ran down her cheeks in a film like the spring water. She thought of the piteous, hideous arms, the pointed white breasts; she put her face in her arms and wept. I have passed the place of the dragon and I can't go back. I have to go on. It was my home, the light in the window, the fire on the hearth, I was a child there, I was the daughter, but it's gone. Now I'm only the dragon's daughter and the king's child, the one that has to go alone, go on, because there is no home behind me.

The water sang, small and fearless. She curled down at last to sleep, worn out. It was a damp place they were in: the touch of the ferns was chill, the ground moist. She could not get warm. There was nothing nearby to build a fire with and she felt too weary, having once half relaxed, to go gather wood and make a fire. Hugh lay fast asleep. He had turned partly onto his face and his arms were drawn in close for warmth. A corner of the red cloak had caught on the ferns and pulled free. She crawled in under it, back to back with Hugh. That was no good. She turned over and put her arm over his side under the fold of the cloak. That was warm, that was comfort. She fell asleep, like a stone falling.

Waking, she lay lapped in warmth some while, rocked in the mild rhythms of Hugh's breathing and her own, entirely tranquil. Memories began to shape themselves, in-truding like the angles and pebbles of the streambed; again she ran down the thin, steep way to the cave mouth, crying defiance, and again, and slipped on the rocks and fell—and sat up, struggling out of the folds of the red cloak. For a while she sat, still sleepy, and looked around at the ferns and the stream, the trees down the gorge, the bluish depths and far ridge lines, the uncolored sky. She crawled over to the stream and crouched to drink where the water rilled over a grey boulder's curve, and washed her face and the back of her neck to clear her mind; then went along the path and off it among the trees to piss. When she came back, Hugh was sitting up huddled in the cloak, hunched over. His thick, rough, fair hair, stiff from her attempt to wash the blood out of it, stuck out from his head; the stubble on his jaw was thick; he looked heavy and haggard. When she asked him how he was it took him a long time to answer. "O.K.," he said. "Cold."

She unwrapped bread and meat for them. She offered him his share, but he did not get his hand out from under the cloak to take it. He hunched up miserably. "Not now," he said.

"Come on. You never ate . . . yesterday, whenever it was."

"Not hungry."

"Drink something anyhow."

He nodded, but did not move to go drink at the stream. After a while he said, "Irena."

"Yes," she said, chewing smoked mutton. She was starv-ing hungry, already eying his untouched share.

"The . . . Where . . ."

"Up there," she said, pointing to the thick-grown slope above the spring. He looked up uneasily.

"Did it . . ."

"It was dead."

Hugh shuddered: she could see the tremor run right through his body. She felt sorry for him, but she was at

161

the moment mainly concerned with food. "Eat something," she said. "It tastes so good. We ought to get going before too long. If you feel all right."

"Going," he repeated.

She attacked a piece of hard dry bread. "Away. Out. To the gate."

He said nothing. He picked up a strip of dried meat, gnawed at it half-heartedly, then gave it up. He went over to the stream to drink. He moved awkwardly, and spent a while levering himself down so that he could drink. He drank for a long time, and finally got up, laborious, holding the red cloak around his shoulders. "I need my shirt or something," he said.

"See if it's dry. I had to wash it. Your coat too."

He looked down at his jeans, stiffened and blackened in streaks with dried blood, and swallowed. "Right. Where is it?" He saw it where she had spread it out over a big fern to dry, and shrugged off the cloak to put the shirt on. Irena watched him, seeing the beauty of his heavy, gleaming arms and throat. Pity and admiration filled her. She said, "You killed the dragon, Hugh."

He finished buttoning the shirt, and after a minute turned towards her. Among the grey boulders and the arching ferns he stood still, and she still between rock and fern, looking at each other.

"You went ahead of me," he said slowly, remaking the moment at the turn of the high path. "You ran down— you called 'Come out.' How did you— What made you do that?"

"I don't know. I was sick of being frightened. I got mad. When I saw the cave. When I saw it I knew she was in it and you'd go in after her, go in there and never come out, and I couldn't stand it. I had to make her come out."

He tucked his shirttail into his jeans, wincing as he moved.

"You call it 'her,' " he said.

162

"It was." She did not want to speak of the breasts and the thin arms.

He shook his head, with a sick look, his pallor increasing. "No, it was— The reason I had to kill it—" he said, and then put out his hand groping for support, and staggered as he stood.

"It doesn't matter. It's dead."

He stood still, his face averted, watching the stream.

"Is the sword . . ."

"The belt and sheath's somewhere here in the ferns. The sword is . . ." She must have looked as sick as he did, for he broke in: "I don't want it."

"Hugh, I think we ought to go on. I want to go. If you're feeling well enough."

"What happened to me, anyway?"

"It fell on you."

He drew a deep breath; his face was bewildered.

"You don't feel like anything got broken or anything?"

"I'm all right. I can't get warm."

"You ought to eat."

He shook his head.

"Maybe we could go, then. It's damp here. Maybe walking will warm you up."

"Right," he said, coming down to where they had slept among the ferns. Irena organised things: strapping the packet of food and the still damp leather coat so that she could carry them easily, and giving Hugh the red cloak. "Put it on right, see, it ties at the neck. I'll carry your coat like this till it dries out." He moved so clumsily that she said, "Is your shoulder all right?"

"Yeah, it's my side, I guess I sprained something."

"What about walking?" she asked sharply, alarmed.

"It'll wear off when I warm up." He was apologetic.

"I don't know where we are," she said.

They stood on the path, just beyond the hands-breadth slip and murmur of the stream crossing and dropping away

163

into fern and moss among tree roots down the mountain-side.

"The only way we could be sure of where we're going would be to follow the whole trail back." She gestured uphill towards the cave. "Past there, and all the way back to the High Step, and then back down to town and onto the south road."

"No," Hugh said.

"Well," she said, much relieved but unable to admit it, "I don't want to either. It was an awfully long way. But I don't know where the gate is from here."

"If we go down," he said, "maybe we'll pick up the sense of the axis, the direction, again."

"O.K. If this is the south side of the mountain we're on, this path leads east. If we can keep going pretty much east or southeast, we ought to cross Third River somewhere down at the foot. And follow Third River to the road; and then on to the gate. It shouldn't be half as long as going clear back around."

He nodded; and she set off down the path under the spindly, crowded firs. She was cheered by walking, cheered by the decision not to go back; she had been afraid he would want to go back. "Go without looking back. . . ."

The white figures stood silent on the dusk road, long ago now, and always, changelessly.

The path was narrow and rocky, a mild downhill grade. It was pleasant to walk, working the knots and sorenesses out of arms and legs, her breath coming easy. All that endless way from the High Step to the cave, all that day or days of being afraid and going on and on, she had not been able to breathe right: there had been a pressure on her lungs from below. Now she felt breathing a pleasure as deep as the pleasure of drinking cool water. I breathe, am breathed, am breath; I am so, am so. So walk, so go on earth, am earth, breath; and beneath all, joy.

They had come a long way when the path reached the

164

bottom of the gorge. It was dark twilight here, a silent creek running under overhanging shrubs and ferns, a slippery dim crossing. Hugh came slowly across. She saw that he did not walk easily. She saw that on this side of the canyon the path turned back, going west.

If it was west.

All confidence slipped from her down in the dark slippery place. If they had come farther than she had counted on, and the cave of the dragon was on the western face of the mountain, then all her directions were off. They were in country she knew nothing about. Anirotembre, the land behind the mountain, the name was all they had ever said of it. If there were towns there they were not spoken of. What had Hugh once said about the west? Something about the sea. That was no good. She must decide what to do. This trail they were on might be a circle. It was the same trail they had been on since they left the High Step, it was the dragon's way. It might go zigzagging in and out of the ravines and up and down the slopes around the mountain and back at last to the High Step. Days walking, maybe, and Hugh already standing here, his head down a bit, glad to stop. It was no good going in circles. They had to get off the dragon's path, and get out.

"I think maybe we should leave the trail here," she said, speaking low, for the deep place was awesome. "We've got to try to keep heading east."

He looked up at the dark slopes overhanging. "It'll be hard to keep any direction, off the trail."

"This river's running east. I think. We can keep following it."

"O.K."

"I'm just guessing it's east," she said shortly. "I don't know."

"There's no way to know." He absolved her without question. "I'd never get anywhere," he said, looking at her across the dark air, "not by myself."

"Out again Brautigan," she said. "Maybe. If only this river is running the right way."

"Not a river at all, it's a creek," he said amiably.

"I call them all rivers. You want to rest here a while?"

"No. Ground's too wet. Let's go on."

It was unnerving to step off the path deliberately, to choose pathlessness, as if you knew your way. At least the going was not hard at first. The trees on this side of the gorge were mostly big old hemlocks, without much underbrush between them, once they were up out of the streambed. The slopes were steep. Before long she wished her right leg could be taken up a couple of inches. But they were making good progress, and there was more light here.

The stream began to descend more steeply. Irena did not try to follow close to the water, but struck up to the spine of the ridge, where the walking was easier and the direction still the same as the flow of water. She had had some hope of seeing the way ahead from the ridgetop, but as always the trees grew too close. Had they been fools to leave the path? Maybe, but she was not turning back. All they could do was take their chance. She was hungry. It seemed too soon to stop, until she thought back to the place below the cave where they had slept—hours ago, way back up the mountain. She turned and said, "I'd like a break," to Hugh, plugging along behind her. He halted promptly. He looked around and pointed out a level bit of ground between the roots of two great, shaggy trees, and they headed for it. He wore the red cloak, which made him look rather like a grandmother from behind, but stately in front view. They found convenient roots to sit on, and Irena unstrapped and unwrapped the packet of food. "I thought maybe we'd go light this time, and next time we stop eat more. Are you very hungry yet?"

"Not hungry at all."

"Eat something, though."

166

She set out portions that looked shamefully meager to her, put up the rest, and fell to. She thought she was chewing slowly and making it last, but it was gone at once, gone before he was half done. He did not even eat the bread. She looked at him uneasily. He was pale, but the haggard look was mostly unshaven beard. His expression was not strained. In fact he looked easy and contented, gazing off among the trees. Evidently feeling her gaze on him, he looked round at her. "You work, or go to school, or what?" he asked.

At first the question seemed crazy, senseless, she could not answer it, here lost on the dragon's mountain. Then the impulse that had moved him asserted itself in her, and she saw nothing strange in what he asked. "I work. Mott and Zerming. I'm an errandperson."

"A who?"

"An errandperson. They have all these affiliates and subsidiaries in town, and a whole lot of correspondence and memos and a lot of blueprints and stuff—they're partly in engineering—and it pays them to use people to carry it around to the different offices instead of using the mail. It's a pretty big outfit. But they're still local and Mr. Zerming still pretty much runs it. He likes to use people who have their own car. But I get all my gas free."

"That's crazy," he said approvingly. "So you drive around all the time?"

"Some of it's easier to do on foot, the downtown offices. Or use the bus. Some days it's all driving. It's kind of weird. I like it because of being on my own and sort of doing it my own way. I hate doing things when somebody else says how to."

"Trouble with most jobs."

"The trouble with this one it's really a kid's job. Sort of unreal—you know. You never really *do* anything. Go and go and go and get nowhere."

"What would you like to do?"

"I don't know. I don't mind this one, you know, it's all right. Just a job. But I guess what a person really does is different. Ought to be different. Like a farm. Or teaching. Or kids. But I'm not there. You have to have some real dirt and a tractor. Or get a teaching degree or a nursing degree or whatever."

"You can go to night school at a community college," he said meditatively. "And work daytime. Starting, anyhow. If . . ."

"That sounds like something you've thought about. Or would you have to go to a special college?"

"What for?"

"Library work, you said."

He looked at her again, a slow look. "That's right," he said, and she knew beyond reason or question that she had recognised something that had been slighted, done something absolutely and permanently right. She did not know what it was, but the effect delighted her. "Crazy," she said. "All those books. What would you do with them, anyhow?"

"I don't know," he said. "Read them?"

His smile was purely good-natured. She laughed. Their eyes met, they both looked away. They were silent for a while.

"If I was just sure we were really going east, I would feel so good! . . . Are you feeling O.K. now?"

"I'm fine."

He always spoke quietly, but she was aware of the resonance of his voice, muted; a beautiful singing voice, it might be.

"Sore as hell here," he remarked with some surprise, exploring his left side with a gingerly touch.

"Let me see."

"It's all right."

"Well, let's see. I thought you moved kind of stiff on that side."

He tried to pull up his shirt but could not raise his left arm. He unbuttoned the shirt. He was embarrassed, and she tried to act detached, doctorly. At the level of the elbow, on the edge of the ribcage, was a greenish-black spot the size of a coffee-can lid. "My God," she said.

"What is it?" he asked, apprehensive; he could not see it clearly.

"A bruise, I guess." She thought of the grip of the sword protruding from the belly of the white creature. Her own body tightened and shrank together at the thought. "From when the—when it fell on you." All around the livid spot the skin was yellowish, and there were other bruises and discolored streaks running up towards the breastbone. "No wonder it feels sore," she said. She felt the heat of the bruise on her fingertips before, very lightly, she touched it.

He caught her hand with his. She thought she had hurt him and looked up into his face. They did not move, she kneeling by him as he sat with one knee drawn up.

"You told me never touch you," he said, his voice husky.

"That was before."

His mouth had softened and slackened, his face was intent, profoundly serious, as she had seen it once before. She had seen on other men's faces that same mask, that made them all alike, and had hidden her own face. Now unafraid, awed but curious, she watched him, and touched his mouth and the hollow of the temple by the eye as gently as she had touched the black bruise, wanting to know this pain and this desire. He held her to him, but awkwardly and timidly, until she put up both her arms, feeling herself go as soft and quick as water. Then he held her and mounted on her, overcoming; yet her strength held and contained his strength.

As he entered her, as she was entered, they came to climax together, and then lay together, mixed and melded, breast against breast and their breath mingled, until he rose in her again and she closed on him, the long pulse of joy enacting them.

He lay there, eyes shut and head turned aside, three-quarters naked, his jeans pulled down. She touched the long splendid line from hip to throat, looked at the peculiarly innocent, fair silky hair in the pit of his arm. "You're cold," she said, and managed to get the red cloak pulled over them as they lay. "You're beautiful," he said, his hands trying to describe that beauty in caresses, but without urgency, tenderly, sleepily. He lay with his face against her shoulder. Half asleep, she saw the unmoving leaves of the hemlocks against the quiet sky. The comfort they gave each other was very great, but it was all the comfort they had. The ground was rough. She felt shivering go through him as he slept. She drew away from him. He protested, saying her name, relapsing for a minute into sleep.

She pulled on her clothes, shivering a bit herself, and as he roused she got him to wear the leather coat, which had finally got fairly dry, and the cloak on top of that. "It's shock that makes you feel cold," she said.

"The shock of what?" he asked with a placid smile.

"Shut up. It does make you cold—shock from injury."

"I think we figured out how to get warm."

"Yes, all right, but we can't get to the gateway by lying here and screwing, Hugh."

"I don't know if we can get there by standing up and walking," he said. "At least we can enjoy the rest stops," he added, and then looked at her to make sure he had not hurt her feelings or offended against modesty. His own modesty, his vulnerability, were entirely admirable to her. She was much cruder than he was, she thought, and if he judged her he must disapprove; but he did not judge her. He did not come to her with judgments, or with a place for her or a name or a use for her. He came with nothing at all but strength and need.

He was looking at her. He said, "Irena, you know, that

170

was the best thing that ever happened to me."

She nodded, unable to answer.

"I suppose we ought to go on," he said. He felt his left side with a thoughtful and disgusted expression. "Wish that would wear off."

"It'll take a while. It's an awful bruise."

He was looking at her again, uncertainly; then, with resolution, came to her, touched her hair and cheek, and kissed her mouth—not expertly, and not very passionately; but it was their first kiss. Better than the kiss she liked the touch of his large hand. She wanted to tell him that he was beautiful and that she liked him, but she was no good at saying things.

"Are you warm enough?" he asked. "I've got all the clothes on."

"I always warm up right away walking."

He waited for her to start off, making no pretense of knowing where they should go. She set off with a new access of confidence along the ridgetop, continuing their course beside the stream in the direction she was resolved to call east.

They walked steadily without speaking for a long way. The ridge, a long, lean spur of the mountain, curved somewhat to the left as they went; its back rose and fell, but the slant over all and always was downhill. The woods on the spine of the ridge were sparse, making easy going, and there were some long open stretches where it was pleasant to walk in the short, dry, brownish grass out from under the dark overhang of branches. At last the spur began to descend steeply, then abruptly. Failing to find an easier way they had to scramble down, clutching at roots and forced sometimes to slide. They fetched up at the bottom, in the streambed, a steep-sided, thickly overgrown ravine. They made their way at once down to the stream to drink.

Irena climbed back up the muddy bank to a clear place made by the falling of a big tree, and stood there consider-

171

ing. This stream was about the same size as Third River. If it was Third River, all they had to do was follow it and they would cross the south road— But this wasn't Third River. This was the same stream they had been following all the way from its source, the spring among the ferns, below the dragon's cave. It was flowing east or southeast, down off the mountain, in this canyon. Third River flowed west, past the mountain. This must be a tributary; it would meet Third River somewhere. It was running toward the left and Third River would run to the right, from this side, if she was facing south now—

She stood trying to work this out, how the streams could be running opposite ways, what direction she must be facing. A knot came into her throat. The names of the compass, north, west, south, east, were words without meaning. Whichever way she faced could be south. Or could be north.

Hugh came up beside her. "You ready for a break?" he asked. He put his hand on her shoulder. She flinched away from the touch.

He moved away at once, crossing the little clearing. He sat down with his back against the massive trunk of the fallen tree, and closed his eyes.

When she came to sit down by him he said, "Maybe we should eat something."

She opened the pack and laid out the food that was left. There was more than she had thought; certainly enough to get by another day on. That gave her courage to say, "I don't know where we are."

"We never did, did we?" he said, impassive. Then, with visible effort, he moved, opened his eyes, asked questions and made suggestions. They discussed following this stream on as they had been doing, since it must join one of the larger streams eventually.

"Or if we're going the wrong way we'll come to the sea," he said, meaning to joke, but his voice died off on the last word.

"The other possibility would be to turn left here," Irena said, working on a second strip of mutton jerky and feeling enlivened by it. "Because I keep thinking we aren't going east enough. And so long as we stay on the mountain we aren't completely lost—at least we know where the mountain is."

"But we don't get any nearer the gateway."

"I know. But the mountain is really the only landmark we have. Since we lost the sense of where the gateway is."

"I know. It's all alike. Like when I went past the gateway. I guess . . . I guess what I'm afraid of is that that's happened again. The gate isn't there any more. There's nothing to find."

"That's never happened to me," she said, defiant. "It's not going to. I'm not going to stay here."

He was pushing fir needles into patterns on the ground beside the fallen tree.

"That's yours," she said, trying to keep her eyes off his share of meat.

"I'm not really hungry."

After a while she said, "You're not leaving more for me, or something creepy like that, are you?"

"No," he said, candid, startled; he smiled, looking up at her. "I just don't feel like eating. If I did you wouldn't stand a chance."

"You can't fast and do a long walk like this too."

"Sure. Live off my fat, like a camel."

She frowned. She wanted to move closer beside him and touch him, his rough hair and tired, stubbly cheeks, his big, powerful, yet childlike hand; but she was prevented by having flinched away from his touch a few minutes before. She wanted to deny his self-denigration but did not know what to say.

His eyes were closed or closing; he had leaned back against the fallen tree. She said nothing, locked in self-consciousness and a deepening depression of spirits. When she glanced at him again he was asleep, his face slack, the hand on his thigh lax.

They ought to go on. They had to go on. They couldn't sit down and sleep, or they would never get to the gateway. "Hugh," she said. He did not hear. Then her anxiety melted in the fearful, passionate tenderness it had risen from. She went to him and pushed him over gently to make him lie down. He roused. "Go to sleep," she said. He obeyed her. She sat beside him a while. As she sat she listened to the sound of the stream nearby, which she had not paid attention to before. It ran quiet here, flowing softly on sand or mud, the gentlest murmur. She began to realise that she was tired. She got the red cloak, which he had not worn once he had warmed up in the leather coat, and put it over them both as a blanket, and fitted herself against Hugh, and went to sleep.

When they roused up both of them were stiff, slow, unready. Irena went back down the bank to drink from the stream. She washed her hands and face, and the cool water was so pleasant, and she felt so ingrained with travel-dirt, that she found a shallow pool downstream and took off her clothes and bathed. She was shy of Hugh's seeing her, and got dressed again quickly. He came down the bank farther upstream, where it was low, and knelt ponderously to drink. "Have a swim. I did," Irena called, buttoning up her shirt, shivering pleasantly.

"Too cold."

"You still feel cold?" she asked, joining him on the ferny, muddy shore.

"All the time."

"It was that—the dragon thing— It was cold. I felt it."

"I just want to see the sunlight," he said. There was a ring of despair in his voice that frightened her.

"We'll get out, Hugh. Don't—"

"Which way?" he asked, standing up. He used a knotty

bush growing from the bank to help pull himself upright.

"Follow the stream, I guess."

"Good. I don't feel much like mountain climbing," he said with an effort at jocularity.

She took his hand. It was stone cold.—Cold from the water, she realised: but that cold touch had shocked her beyond the reach of rational explanation. She was in fear for him. She looked up at him and said his name.

He met her gaze, looking at her as if he saw all of her with a longing he could not speak. He put his right hand on her hair and drew her against him. He was a wall, a fortress, a bulwark, and mortal, frail, easier to hurt than heal; dragonkiller, child of the dragon; king's son, poor man, poor, brief, unknowing soul. His desire for her stood up and throbbed against her belly, but his arms held her in a greater longing even than that, one for which life cannot give consummation. She held him so to her, they stood there together.

9

She led the way. He came along as well as he could. She looked back often, and sometimes had to wait for him. He tried to keep up, but the going was not easy along the stream bank. Roots, bushes, ferns crowded together and the ground beneath them was uneven, sometimes slippery. Since he had pulled something wrong, coming down the steep ravine, the pain in his side never left off any more. It shortened his breath and his stride. After a while he did not think about trying to keep up but only about trying to keep going. Where a lesser stream came down into the one they were following it spread out into a marsh where there was no sound footing, and they decided they would have to cross the water. That was very difficult. The dizziness that came and went in his head made it hard to balance on the slick stones against the tug of the current. He was afraid that if he fell he would pull something wrong there again in his side. He got across all right, but a while later they had to cross again, he did not know why; he was concentrating entirely now on the next few steps. She tried to give him a hand, crossing, but it wasn't much good. She wasn't big enough, if he slipped he slipped, damned elephant. The water was burning cold. They were across now, and an easier way opened along a sandy shore under grey trees. If only his side didn't burn, and the sword drive into him a little deeper now, and again now, and again now. She was like a shadow, she went before him so lightly; the only shadow in this world without shadows, without moon or sun. Wait for me, Irena! he wanted to say, but he didn't have to; she waited. She turned to him, returned to him. Her warm, strong hand touched his. "You want to rest a while, Hugh?" He shook his head. "I want to go on," he said. The sword drove into him a little deeper, again, now. His name, his father's name, which he had hated, in her voice was baptism: a breath, the outbreath: you. You my fulfillment. You beyond all expectation met: you my life. Not death but life. Before the cave of the dragon we were married.

"For a little while," he said. He was on his knees. She came to him, faithful and concerned. He told her not to worry, he wanted to sit down and rest for a little while, or he meant to tell her that.

She made him lie down, and put the red cloak around him; she held him and tried to warm him with her warmth. It was he that was the shadow, she was warmth, sunlight.

"Sing the song," he said.

She did not hear him at first; he could not speak loudly because of the sword in his side. When he said it again she understood. She propped herself up on her elbow and turned her face away a little and sang in her thin, sweet voice, the lark's voice, without fear,

> When the flower is in the bud
> and the leaf is on the tree
> the lark will sing me home
> to my ain countrie.

"It's that one," he said.

"What is it?"

"Home's that country," he said. "Not this one."

Her face was close to his, and she stroked his hair. Her warmth had come into him. He closed his eyes. When he woke whatever was wrong in his side did not hurt at all, until he moved. Getting up was the hardest part. He could not kneel down to the water to drink without having to get up all over again, ashamed of the noises that came out of his chest as he did so, a series of creaking gasps, but he couldn't stand up without making them. "Come on," Irena said, "along here." She spoke so reassuringly that he asked, "You found the way?" She did not hear him. He could walk all right, but he stumbled a lot. It worked best if she walked with him. She guided him so well that he could walk with his eyes shut part of the time, but when he staggered off the path he pulled her with him, so he tried to keep his eyes open. The going was easy. The trees parted before them, made way for them. But they had to cross the creek again. It was not possible.

"You did it before," she said.

Had he? That would be why he felt so cold: he was wet. No harm to get wet again, then. The water burned like fire, the dark, quick-running water he would not drink again. There was the shelf-rock above the creek where he, where she had knelt. And the bushes and the flowerless grass of the glade, the beginning place, but the end, now; and the pine and the high laurels, but no way between them, not till her hand opened it for him. But still he could not go through it till she took his hand and came beside him into the new world.

She had expected sunlight. She had always thought they would come out into the hot, tremendous sunlight of that hot summer. They came across the threshold into night and rain.

The rain was falling thick in big drops. The sound of it hitting the leaves of the woods and the ground was beautiful, and the smell of it. Her face was wet with rain as if with tears. But she could not let Hugh rest, as she had counted on doing as soon as they got through. Not on this soaked ground, and their jeans and shoes already wet through from crossing the three rivers. They had to keep on going. It wasn't fair, he was blind with pain and fever. But she kept hold of his arm and he kept going. They worked their way slowly through the dark wood, and out across the waste fields. Air and ground were streaked by turning distant carlights from the highway fanning out through the falling rain. Once Hugh stumbled and as he recovered himself, pulling heavily on her, cried out; but then he said, "It's all right," and they went on, getting closer to the gravel road, the all-night lights beside the paint factory their beacon. On the short slope up to the road he sank down onto his knees and then without any word or sign slipped forward and lay face down on the ground.

She had come down with him; she crouched beside him in the wet grass. After a while she scrambled up onto the road's edge, stood there a moment looking back at the darkness where he lay. She could not see him. Whimpering with misery as he had whimpered with pain, she started to walk down the road, towards the farm.

Headlights behind her, from the factory. In rabbit terror she froze on the road's edge, heard the engine slow, the tires grate.

"Hey. Anything wrong?"

That it might yet be, that it might always be what she feared she knew, but she turned around and went to the car. She was shaking. She made out a redbearded face in the back glow of the lights. "My friend's hurt," she said.

"Where? Hang on."

It was a small car, and Hugh never came to enough to be much help, but Redbeard, determined, got him folded somehow into the front seat, then jack-knifed Irena into the back and drove at eighty and enjoying it to Fairways Hospital. He was out of the car as he jammed on the brake at the emergency entrance, enjoying that too. Once Hugh had been taken in the glamorous part was over, but still Redbeard waited with her in the emergency waiting room, got her coffee and a candy bar from the machines in the lobby, did what a fellow human being might do; not an uncommon thing, in Irena's experience, nor yet, nor ever, a common one. It is royalty that call each other sister, brother.

The doctor that talked to her at last asked a few questions. Irena had been listening to Redbeard talking basketball scores and had prepared no story. "He got beat up," she said, all she could think of when she realised there had to be some explanation.

"You were in the woods," the doctor said.

"Hiking."

"You got lost? How long have you been there?"

"I don't know exactly."

"I'd better have you checked over."

"I'm all right. Just tired. I was scared."

"You're certain you weren't hurt yourself?" the doctor said harshly: a middle-aged woman, tired, grey-faced in the merciless fluorescent light of the ten P.M. Labor Day weekend hospital emergency ward hallway.

"I'm O.K., I'll be fine when I get some sleep. Is Hugh—"

"Have you somewhere to go?"

"The man that picked us up, he'll drive me to my mother's place. Is Hugh—"

"I'm waiting for the X-rays. He'll stay here. Did you sign those—yes. All right." She turned away. Cowed by the power of the Doctor, the Hospital, Irena turned to go in silence.

The orderly who had taken Hugh in looked out of a cubicle. "He asked would somebody get in touch with his mother," he said, seeing Irena. "You do that?"

"Yes."

"He's all right," the doctor said. "Go get some sleep."

"They're going to keep you another night."

"I know," he said, lying comfortably on the high hard bed, the next to last of the ward. "I don't feel a whole lot like getting up right now anyhow."

"But are you O.K.?"

"Fine. They got all this stuff wrapped around me, look. No, I can't show you, this thing opens in the back, it's indecent. But there's all this bandage stuff around me, like a mummy. Every time I wake up I get a pill."

"It's a broken rib?"

"One broken and one cracked. How about you?"

"I'm fine. Listen, Hugh, have they asked you about, you know, what happened?"

"I just said I didn't remember."

"That's good. See, if we had different stories they might think there was something fishy."

"What did happen?"

"We were hiking in the woods and some tough guys beat you up and then ran."

"Was that it?"

He saw her uncertainty.

"Irena. I do remember."

She smiled, still uncertain. "I thought you were spaced out on those pills, maybe."

"I am. Mostly just sleepy. I guess there's parts . . . I don't know how we got to the gate. We did get onto the right path finally?"

"Yeah. You were kind of out of it." She put her hand on his. They were both made shy by the other people in the restless, busy ward, men in bed, half-dressed, swathed heads, bare feet sticking out of casts, sleeping, staring, visitors coming and going, television and radios on three different stations and the smell of death and disinfectant.

"Did you have to go to work today?"

"No. It's still only Monday."

"My God."

"Listen, Hugh."

He smiled, watching her.

"I went and saw your mother, this morning."

After a minute he asked rather vaguely, "She all right?"

"When I called her last night, you know, she didn't seem to understand very well. She kept asking who I was, and I said I'd been hiking with you, you know, but she kept asking the same things. She was upset. It was late, and everything. I shouldn't have called. So when they wouldn't let me in here this morning I thought I ought to go see her. She didn't seem to understand you were here, in the hospital."

He said nothing.

"Well, she . . ."

"She jumped on you," he said, with so much anger that she hurried to speak—"No, she didn't— Only she didn't seem to— Well, I said you needed some clothes and stuff. I thought she'd want to take them to you, you know. She went and came back with this suitcase, she had it all ready, it's in the car, I'll leave it for you. I— Well, she sort of shoved it at me, at the door, and said, 'He doesn't have to come back after this,' and she was—she shut the—I couldn't do anything but just go. After what, did she mean? I must have said something all wrong and she misunderstood and I don't know what to, how to straighten it out. I'm sorry, Hugh."

"No," he said. He closed his eyes. Presently he turned his hand, gripping Irena's hand strongly. "It's all right," he said when he could speak. "Home free."

"But doesn't she want you to come back?" Irena said in distress and perplexity.

"No. And I don't want to. I want to go with you. I want to live with you." He sat up to get his head closer to her. "I want to get a place, an apartment or something, if you— I have some money in the bank, if this damned hospital doesn't take it all— If you—"

"Yes, all right, listen. I wanted to tell you. After I saw her it still wasn't visiting hours yet, so I went out to 48th and Morressey. There was this ad in this morning's paper. That's the Hillside district, you know. It sounded really good, two twenty-five a month with utilities, it's really good for ten minutes from downtown. I went right there. It's a garage apartment. I'll take it anyway. I signed for it. I can't go back where I was."

"You want to take it together?"

"If you want to. It's a really nice place. The people in the house are really nice. They aren't married either."

"We are," he said.

Next morning they left the hospital together. It was raining again, and she wore the patched and battered cloak, he the stained leather coat. They went off in her car together. There is more than one road to the city.